RIVER
FOLK
TALES

OF

BRITAIN
AND
IRELAND

RIVER
FOLK
TALES

OF

BRITAIN
AND
IRELAND

LISA
SCHNEIDAU

The
History
Press

For my godmother, Moira Houghton,
with love

First published 2022

The History Press
97 St George's Place, Cheltenham,
Gloucestershire, GL50 3QB
www.thehistorypress.co.uk

British Library Cataloguing in Publication Data.
A catalogue record for this book is available from the British Library.

ISBN 978 0 7509 9722 5

Typesetting and origination by The History Press
Printed and bound in Great Britain by TJ Books Limited, Padstow,
Cornwall.

Trees for LYfe

CONTENTS

About the Author

Lisa Schneidau is a professional storyteller, sharing stories that inspire, provoke curiosity and build stronger connections between people and nature. Lisa trained as an ecologist. She has worked with wildlife charities all over Britain to restore nature in the landscape, in roles including farm advisor, river surveyor, political lobbyist and conservation director. She lives on Dartmoor.

Acknowledgements

Where possible, I have drawn on multiple story sources for every traditional story retold here. I'm grateful to the folklorists and authors whose work has heavily influenced this book, especially Katherine Briggs and Ruth Tongue. My thanks to the ever-generous and wondrous storytelling community; the audiences and school classes who have listened and shared the stories and given feedback; and all the storytellers who have collected and shared these tales in the telling down the generations. I hope that I have honoured their stories well here and added something useful to the tradition.

Thanks to David Wyatt for his beautiful cover artwork and to Nicola Guy at The History Press for all her support in bringing the book together.

Thanks in particular to Moira Houghton, Sharon Jacksties, Katy Lee, Caroline Preston, Karl Schneidau, Nikki Walsh and Adrian Wolfe; and to Tony Whitehead, who has provided support, encouragement and inspiration throughout.

INTRODUCTION

For they were young, and the Thames was old
And this is the tale that River told …
Rudyard Kipling (1865–1936)

One morning, not so very long ago, I visited a stretch of the upper River Torridge in north Devon. It was a sunny, early autumn day, following two days of heavy rain. As we walked down to the river, the leaves on the trees were just beginning to turn and the robins were tuning up for the winter singing season to come.

I was visiting to see the work done by my Devon Wildlife Trust project team to restore this part of the river channel. In common with most of the country, efficient land drainage to the River Torridge over many decades has led to an increased flow of water, which has scoured out the river bed and carried natural river bed materials downstream. Our work had been to reintroduce many thousands of tonnes of local gravel to the river, recreating a diversity of structure that would benefit many river species. The landowner was proud of the work and excited to see how the river would change over time.

It was an extraordinary sight. The work had only been completed two days before our visit, and the river was already busy with the introduced material, carving meanders and excavating pools into its course. It was a great success; but there was a problem. The river water was brown, and it stank of slurry, rain-washed from the land of the neighbouring farmers upstream.

That site visit demonstrated an important fact: rivers are complicated. A river is not just a channel of water, it is part of an entire water system involving the sky, the land and the sea. Rivers reflect back what we put into the water and what we take out. My little story may yet turn out to be a happy ending for a wilder River Torridge, but clearly there is still more work to be done, more demons to be battled and more lessons to be learned, there and in many other places.

Britain and Ireland hold over 4,000 miles of watercourse, depending on how you define a river. From source to babbling brook, down through flood plain to the sea, our rivers are the lifeblood of our landscape, shaping our environment and being shaped in turn.

However, the untamed and changing nature of our rivers has been manipulated by people over many centuries, from the time that water was used to transport the Stonehenge sarsens over 6,000 years ago. Rivers clean, drain, wash and dilute; they transport us, create energy and give us water to irrigate crops. Rivers soothe us, inspire us and give us space to play.

The result is that there are no rivers in Britain and Ireland that can be claimed as completely natural or wild. Some rivers are now no more than large industrial drains, while others are choked with sediment and nutrients from intensive farming, sewage outflow and industry. Stocks of salmon and trout are in sharp decline. Recent monitoring figures from the respective organisations managing rivers in Britain and Ireland are not an encouraging read. A total of 65.7 per cent of water bodies in Scotland, 52.8 per cent in the Republic of Ireland, 40 per cent in Wales, 31 per cent in Northern Ireland and just 16 per cent of water bodies in England were in good ecological status in 2018 and 2019.

We are getting something very wrong with our rivers, and yet they can still bite back. The number of storms and floods will increase as the effects of climate change begin to hit us. As water rushes down through denuded catchments that cannot soak it up, the same voices that want to dredge, engineer and control our rivers will only get louder in response. Happily, there are also many organisations and landowners working hard to restore our rivers and use nature to help us manage flood water and pollution; but, as the project above has shown, they are often constrained and frustrated by the sheer complexity of issues across our watery landscape that need to be tackled.

Perhaps the real culprit, the real missing piece of the jigsaw, is our personal connection to rivers, or lack of it. How many of us spend any time during our daily routine with a river or its wildlife? Cross a river or use a river to transport ourselves from one place to the next? Think about the water that comes out of our taps? Find time in our busy lives to stop and notice?

Yet sogginess seeps through the imaginations and very souls of the people living in the islands of Britain and Ireland. We love to complain about too much rain, and some artists say their creative muse cannot survive without it. We still revere holy wells with their miracle-inducing waters, visit spas, and when we travel we notice our tea tastes different because of a change in the water.

Our culture and language journey with rivers. We talk of a flow of inspiration and imagination, and what might be hidden under the surface. Rivers take away the old and wash us clean. We acknowledge the power of rivers, and walk alongside them to find peace, but we never want to invoke their wrath; we wonder at the river's journey to the sea, travelling to wide expanse and endless possibility.

I've worked in nature conservation of rivers in Britain for twenty-five years now, and so it was inevitable that I became curious about rivers in the myths, fairy tales and folk tales of Britain and Ireland. When I started my own river journey, I wanted to know about the archetypes contained in our river stories. How is our complex relationship with rivers reflected back to us in folk tale form? How connected are these stories with actual places? Is there inspiration to be found here, about how we can meet the challenges of honouring our rivers and the wildlife they support? Is there courage in these stories to provoke action, in the face of a climate and ecological emergency where flood risk is increasing for many?

This book is the result. Here are my own versions of thirty-two traditional tales, about rivers, lakes, bogs and wells, from Britain and Ireland. I have chosen this geography because water doesn't respect political borders, and because of the ways in which the cultures of our countries share a common heritage.

I am a great believer in re-wilding storytelling, and I have worked to honour these stories while bringing them alive in the context of nature and place. Some stories are more archetypal, and these have provided their own nature connections as I have worked with them.

I have hunted out stories from many different sources: folklore archives and collections, natural history literature, and of course listening to storytellers. Some tales are well known, others more obscure. Like all storytellers, I am grateful to those who have collected and told these stories all down the generations, known and unknown. I have tried wherever possible to pursue a story back to its oldest referenced source. A list of story sources and further reading is provided.

I have told many of these stories to different audiences, indoors and out in the field, sharing ideas and emotions that the stories provoke. Folk tales have their own personalities and idiosyncrasies. Some are darker than others, and the teller will need to decide which stories to share with very young ones.

Dip your toes in the water now, and immerse yourself in these stories of rivers, bogs, lakes, wetlands and wells. I hope they will inspire you and provoke curiosity about this essential aspect of the landscape of Britain and Ireland. They will show you the role of water in our past, and hint at something of our relationship with the water environment in the future.

Enjoy reading these tales, and do try telling them out loud to others. After that, why don't you go to seek out your local river and its very own version of watery magic?

1

SACRED BEGINNINGS

All was a-shake and a-shiver – glints and gleams and
sparkles, rustle and swirl, chatter and bubble.

Kenneth Grahame,
from The Wind in the Willows *(1908)*

Have you ever stopped to wonder where all that river water
comes from, flowing through seasons and years and ages,
and how many people have stopped and wondered at the
same thing?

The water of rivers must begin somewhere, whether it's
bubbling from a spring, oozing from a peatland pool or
seeping through a chalk aquifer. From there on, a seemingly
endless flow of water makes its way down to the wide ocean,
carving out the land as it goes, shifting shape over time.

Of course, rivers are not a linear matter; they are part of
the great cycle of water that includes land, sky, the oceans
and all living things. But where rivers spring from the land,
there is magic to be found.

Similar motifs echo through the folk tales of Britain and
Ireland: the coming of a great flood; the direction of giants in
shaping the land with water; and feminine wisdom, flowing
like emotion and bringing life to the land all around.

Fintan mac Bochra

Fintan mac Bochra first appears in the Lebor Gabala Erenn (Book of Invasions) *from the twelfth century, which attempts to put ancient Irish history into a Biblical context. He is a compelling father figure for Ireland, and the only Irishman to survive the great flood. 'Bochra' may refer to his mother, or just to the sea in general, but some suggest that Fintan's mother was Banba, one of the three ancient land goddesses of Ireland.*

The Hill of Tounthinna overlooks the River Shannon, near Portroe, County Tipperary. A kype is the hooked mouthpart of a male salmon at breeding time.

This is my own interpretation of how these snippets of ancient Irish folklore might play out in story form.

Fintan mac Bochra was one of the first people ever to set eyes on the beautiful Emerald Isle, and it was just as well, for he had the eyes, the ears and the heart of a poet. Some say that he was a lucky man to be on the boat that sailed there, because there were only three men but fifty women. Fintan chose Cesair, daughter of Banba, for his wife, but when they all landed and set about making a life for themselves, there was little time to sort out the imbalance between men and women.

It was only the second full moon after they had landed when the tidal wave hit their little settlement, and it showed little mercy. That morning Fintan had travelled inland and uphill to forage. When the water hit, he was in a little cave in the hill that would come to be called Tounthinna. That journey saved his life. Later that afternoon Fintan walked down from the hill and over the brow towards home, but instead of the comforting sight of huts and buildings and home fires, the wide ocean met him far too soon; the sea had eaten the land, and it had swallowed everything. All his companions had perished, and Fintan was alone in a strange place.

He stood at the edge of the water, overwhelmed with sorrow, and tears welled in his eyes. 'As if there wasn't enough water already,' said Fintan mac Bochra. 'The whole world has turned to water, and I with it.'

There was magic in his words. Fintan's eyes shifted to the side of his head, his neck folded into silver flaps as his arms became fins and his legs fused into a tail. Fintan leapt into the air and down into the water, a sleek, scaly salmon. And that is how Fintan mac Bochra survived the great flood.

Who knows what Fintan saw of their old settlement under the waves, or whether he ever saw his wife Cesair again? He stayed a salmon for a whole cycle of the sun, flashing silver in the rivers and travelling thousands of miles through the northern seas.

That is how Fintan got to know the life of the rivers of Ireland.

The next summer, Fintan the salmon was leaping a waterfall on the Shannon when, mid-air, his fins broadened and turned tawny, his great kype transformed into a hooked beak, and his eyes became black and beady. Fintan the eagle shook the last beads of river water from his feathers and flew up into the heavens. He soared across the blue skies that day to the mountains of the west.

Fintan the eagle explored the island of Ireland from north to south, and from east to west. He saw all the great rivers of Ireland from his bird's-eye view. He saw the River Bann, the Barrow, and the Blackwater; the Boyne, the Erne, the Shannon and the Nore; the loughs at the coast and the loughs inland. He learned the play of nature in these great bodies of water, the creatures that needed their gifts and those who could be preyed upon.

That is how Fintan understood the flow of the rivers of Ireland.

The next summer, Fintan the eagle was restless. He was chasing a raven through the valleys one morning when, drawing a deeper breath than normal, he felt his wings shrink back, his body compact, and his skull tighten. Fintan the eagle became Fintan the peregrine falcon, diving for cover; and it was all he could do to escape the mobbing from two very amused ravens that day.

Fintan the falcon roamed the length and breadth of Ireland, his keen eyes observing everything on the land, and how the wild creatures were faring. He noticed more humans settling as the waters receded, and animals kept within fences; he saw wagons and chariots, and great battles between clans, then the crows making their feasts. He observed new clans arriving from across the sea, as old clans made use of some of their magic and forgot the rest.

That is how Fintan learned the stories of the rivers of Ireland.

One morning the next summer, Fintan woke and found himself curled up high in a tree, but without feathers to warm his toes or the wings to reach the ground. Fintan was back in his human form. He had to edge along the branch of the great tree he was in and climb clumsily to safety on the ground.

Fintan, now eighteen years of age, started his new journey as a man. He walked all the ancient paths of Ireland, and he saw many tribes gain power and fall in their turn. He met a great and fearless leader to the north, a hound of men with a hero light around his head. He helped a great leader to the south, a man with fairy blood who led a famous war band and who gained all the knowledge there was to know in the world.

That is how Fintan could tell the fate of the rivers of Ireland.

But something even more magical happened to Fintan: he never seemed to age, as he watched everything birth and live and perish around him. Some say that Fintan lived for many thousands of years, and that he knew the rivers and islands of Ireland and their poetry better than any man alive or dead.

One day, on the island of Achill in the county of Mayo, Fintan met a hawk perching on the low branch of a rowan tree, and he smiled, for he knew what it felt like to be this creature. The hawk's feathers were battered and scruffy, but his eyes were bright.

'You made it, then,' said the Hawk of Achill.

'If you mean that I have seen many things, then let me tell you, so you may wonder at them,' replied Fintan with a grin, and he sat down beside the hawk and started to tell his stories.

'Yes, I was there too,' said the hawk, when Fintan told of the heroes of Ireland.

'Yes, I was there too,' he said when Fintan described the war bands and the tribes and the magic.

'Yes, I was there too, when they were written,' he said, after Fintan had recited all of the ancient Irish poetry he had heard (which was to say, all the Irish poetry that ever existed).

'Yes, I saw that, and it was lucky I could fly,' said the hawk when Fintan told him of the tidal wave, the great flood, and the death of his wife Cesair.

'Then we are about the same great age, you and I?' asked Fintan.

'About 5,500 years old apiece, I reckon,' said the hawk. 'But let me tell you of something now. Have you heard of St Patrick, and of the new religion – that of Christ?'

The hawk told Fintan what he knew.

'So, our time is done, and our stories must end here,' said Fintan.

Fintan and the hawk died then, under the shade and the protection of the rowan tree. But they didn't die completely, because now their stories have travelled to you.

TAMARA, TAVY AND TORRIDGE

The huge granite mass of Dartmoor, in Devon, is sometimes called 'the mother of rivers'. The moor is full of treacherous peatlands, with few places as bleak as Cranmere Pool, a good 16-mile round trip from where I am writing. Cranmere used to be a deep pool of water, and a wild ghost called Benjie is still said to be working there, doomed for eternity to try and empty the pool with a sieve. The rivers Torridge (East Okement tributary),

Tavy and Dart all start near Cranmere Pool. Of the rivers in this story, the Torridge flows north, picking up other parts of the river from the north-west coast of Devon, until it meets the sea at Braunton. The Tavy flows south-west and meets the Tamar at Plymouth Sound. You'll find a story from the River Dart later in this book.

The River Tamar, or 'great water', first recorded by Ptolemy in the second century, begins elsewhere. It rises on Wooley Moor at Morwenstow to the north, with Bodmin Moor in the west and Dartmoor in the east. The Tamar forms part of the boundary between Devon and Cornwall.

This origin tale of Tamara, originally written in Victorian times, is a classic part of every storyteller's repertoire in Devon and Cornwall. It has been the topic of many a conversation with fellow storytellers, but it has taken me a long time and a lot of trial and error to find a version I like telling! Given I have worked on the Torridge and Taw for many years and live in Dartmoor National Park – and dance 'Tamara' with Beltane Border Morris – it would be rude not to.

In the earliest days, the cold days, there were no people in the islands of Britain, and there were no trees. Those were the times when – if you had been there – you could see the bones of the land sticking out, and when giants carved up the landscape and hurled rocks around for fun. But the giants weren't the only spirits who loved the land. The little, homely earth spirits lived in burrows in the lower, softer ground, and very rarely went above the surface, because it was cold and dangerous. They clung to the security of their earthy caverns and tunnels, dank with peat and thick with magic.

But young spirits always want to explore. That was the case with young Tamara, an earth spirit who was born north-west of the great moor, just as the earth was warming. She was never content with staying underground in safety – there was too much of the world to see.

'Don't stay up there for too long,' Tamara's father would say. 'The giants will crush you, and the sun will burn you all away.'

'Just for a little time, father, I'll be back soon. It's all so *serious* underground,' she said, and flashed him a smile.

The days came and went. For Tamara, a little time became a longer time, and a longer time became a whole day above ground. She was fascinated with the roof of the sky, the brightness of the sun, and the sparkle it made in the stones; she would make up stories as she danced across the plains. Her father pleaded and scolded, but it made no difference.

One day, Tamara dared to climb to the high rocks, where the stones glittered, and birds of prey screeched high above. She noticed the sun was hanging low in the west, and was just turning to go back, when a huge rock sailed over her head and landed a little way in front of her with a crash.

'Sorry!' said a gruff voice. As the ground shook with every step, a young giant ambled towards her, grinning with curiosity. 'Ain't you the pretty one!' he said. 'Tavy the giant at your service – but you mustn't tell on me.'

'Tell on you?' asked Tamara.

'Me dad,' said Tavy. 'He hates me talking to spirits. Says you'll fill my head with nonsense.'

Tamara laughed merrily. 'Perhaps I will! But my dad told me you'd squash me flat.'

Tavy and Tamara became firm friends, and it wasn't long before another young giant, Torridge, joined them as they roamed across the high moor. Most days, whenever she could get away, Tamara climbed the steep slope to the wide, rocky land, and she danced and joked with the giants up there on the roof of the world. She needed to take five steps to cover each lumbering footfall of the young giants, but she led them a merry chase across the rocks, and she left Tavy and Torridge starry-eyed for their new friend.

Tamara's father noticed that she was absent from home for longer and longer, and one day he lost his temper with her. 'You're staying underground today,' he shouted. 'You're grounded.'

Up on the high moor, Tavy and Torridge waited for Tamara, but she didn't appear.

'P'raps she's getting fed up with you,' Tavy joked to Torridge.

'What do you mean?' cried Torridge. 'Tamara favours me, I tell you. I've been thinking of marriage!'

'Not if I have anything to do with it!' roared Tavy. 'She's mine!'

A fight between giants is not a pretty sight. Usually, giants try to solve disputes with friendly games, like quoits or hurling; but when they get violent, giants scoop up the rocks with their hands, take aim at each other, and leave the land in ruin behind them. Tavy and Torridge began to fight, and both got bruised quickly, because the rocks of Dartmoor are very, very hard.

'Stop,' cried Torridge, nursing a large bump on the top of his head. 'I've got an idea. Why don't we go to ask Tamara which one of us she prefers?'

'Good idea,' growled Tavy. 'As long as the answer is – me.'

They both strode across the moor to the north-west, where Tamara had told them she lived, until they nearly reached the coast. The ground crashed and rumbled with every step they took, and Tamara, safe underground, could tell there were giants approaching. While her father's back was turned, she darted out above the ground.

'Tavy! Torridge!' she whispered. 'Go back! Don't let my father find out you're here!'

But it was too late. Tamara's father was already standing behind her. He scattered earth magic on the two young giants, and instantly they were fast asleep and snoring.

'Now then, my girl,' said her father. 'Get back underground while you are safe!'

Tamara took a deep breath. Tears were streaming down her face.

'Father, these giants are not dangerous,' she said. 'They are my friends. I'm staying here above ground with them.'

Her father's face was as red as molten lava. 'You dare to disobey me again, daughter? Very well. If you insist on being wilful, I will let you wander the earth above ground forever.'

He raised his hands and muttered a simple incantation, and Tamara disappeared.

At the spot where Tamara had stood, a little spring of water bubbled up out of the ground. The water seeped across the soil, and quickly gathered itself into a little channel of water bubbling between the grassy tussocks and the heather.

Tamara the stream flowed south, widening and deepening, carving her way across the soil and the rock, tumbling and playing with the stones. The sun flashed and shimmered on her water as she broadened into a great river, dancing and running across the land. All manner of creatures ran and slithered and crawled to explore this new wonder of Tamara

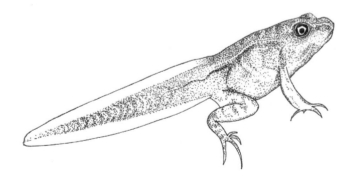

the river. She flowed south until she met the coast and her water danced with the salt and the great unknown ocean.

It was several hours later that Tavy awoke, cold and hungry, and he saw Tamara the spring in front of him, her father nowhere to be seen. Tavy tried to hold the water of the spring in his hands and watched the beauty of the light on the rippling surface. His friend was transformed, she had found a new game, and he wanted to be with her more than anything in the world.

Tavy ran home to his own family on the high moor, but by the time he got there the news had already spread. Tavy's father was angry with him for disobeying him, but when he saw how unhappy his son was, and how much he wanted to join Tamara, he took pity, and cast his own magic. Tavy disappeared, and a little spring of water bubbled out of a bog on the high moor, flowing south and west as fast as he could to meet his friend.

Tavy the river met Tamara the river close to the sea, and the friends have been together ever since, playing with the stones and the mud and the sand and the sunlight, their water mingling and gliding out to the endless sea beyond.

But what of Torridge?

Torridge slept for a good while longer than his friend. When he woke alone, and saw Tamara the spring, he also ran back, distraught, to his father on the high moor. After much begging and pleading, his father cast the magic and Torridge also became a little bubbling spring on the moor, trickling, burbling, gurgling, racing across the land.

But poor young Torridge had never had much sense of direction. He didn't realise at first, but he was flowing north, down from the high moor, across the clay lands, until he met a different sea to the north of the land that would become Devon. Torridge would never see his beloved Tamara again.

That's how the great rivers Tamar, Tavy and Torridge began.

THE STORY OF SIONNAN

At 224 miles long, the River Shannon is the longest river in Ireland and in the British Isles. It divides Ireland into east and west, with relatively few crossing points, starting at the Shannon Pot below Culicagh Mountain in County Cavan and flowing through or between eleven counties before meeting the estuary at Limerick.

The importance of the Shannon was first recorded by Ptolemy in the second century. There are several myths about how the river began, all of them involving Sionnan, the granddaughter of Manannán mac Lir, god of the sea and ruler of the Otherworld. The notion of a woman or goddess drowning at the head of a river is a common motif in Irish mythology: her power dissolves into the water and brings life and magic to the land. My version of Sionnan's story draws from two poems in the Dindshenchas, or 'lore of places', in early Irish literature.

Traditionally Shannon Pot is also Connla's Well, the otherworldly Irish well of wisdom, although other places also lay claim to the title. 'Connla' means 'great lord' and it's a frequent name in Irish mythology. Given the hazelnuts falling into the water, some texts identify Connla's Well as the pool where the Salmon of Knowledge lived. W.B. Yeats said that Connla's Well was full of the 'waters of emotion and passion, in which all purified souls are entangled'. It's a fitting description for this story.

Sionnan was a graceful woman and skilled at crafts. She was known the length and breadth of Ireland for the quality of her weaving. The fine cloth she made was second to none, and some said it shimmered with more than the flaxen warp and weft, because Sionnan was a granddaughter of Manannán mac Lir himself.

But if you were to meet Sionnan, you would find a very ordinary woman, and you would see no trace of her magical ancestry. She was practical, she was direct, and she thought in very logical ways; the meanders and mysteries of a poet's heart were not available to Sionnan.

As she grew older, as she perfected her craft and brought delight to everyone in Ireland with her cloth, Sionnan started to doubt herself and she felt empty.

'What good are practical things?' she thought. 'Practical things will never tug at the heart or tickle the imagination of the bards, and they will never last. Everything in my life is dull.'

Sionnan decided that she wanted to learn magic, and inspiration, and the divine arts, and she wanted to weave them into her work. She followed her ancestry first, travelling to her grandfather's realm under the sea, the Otherworld itself.

Manannán mac Lir listened gravely to his granddaughter's request and stroked his beard in thought.

'I cannot help you,' he said at last. 'To gain sacred inspiration, you need to access it at the correct place. You need to find the place where the human world and the Otherworld meet directly, and that is at Connla's Well, where the hazel trees give their magic to the water. But mind: you, Sionnan, are not allowed to drink the waters of the well to gain its wisdom. That blessing is only allowed for Nechtan and his three cup-bearers.'

'That's not fair!' cried Sionnan.

'Fair or not, that is the way of things,' said Manannán mac Lir.

Sionnan left the Otherworld with a puzzle muddling her mind. Was it possible for her to gain the sacred inspiration of Connla's Well without drinking its water and angering the gods? She travelled north for a long way before she found the right place, at the foot of a great hill.

Soon, Sionnan was standing before Connla's Well itself, and the clouds in the sky reflected from its shimmering

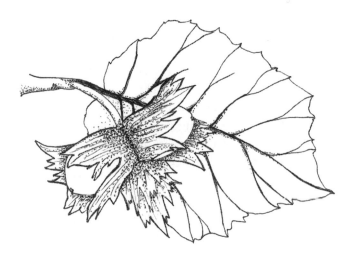

surface as dragonflies darted across the water. Many-branched hazel trees sprouted from the water's edge and leaned suggestively over the pool. But the world underneath the water was a mystery forbidden to her.

Sionnan gazed on the beautiful scene, pushed back her dark hair and sighed. Goodness knows how many hazelnuts had fallen in there over the years, and how much magic the water held. But how could she access just a tiny part of that magic, that inspiration, for herself? There had to be a way.

She knelt on the bank of the pool and looked closer at the water, and then she laughed. Tiny little bubbles were rising from the deep and, one by one, they popped, now there, now gone. A hazelnut floated lazily on the water, a mass of little bubbles. Here was the place where the air met the water, in miniature. Sionnan was entranced. She started playing with the bubbles, catching them on her fingers before they disappeared.

Sionnan leaned further in, and further, until the inevitable happened – she lost her balance, and fell into the water. She scrabbled for a foothold, but there was none, and she could not swim. Sinking beneath the surface, flailing wildly, she took a huge gulp of water.

At that moment, Sionnan angered the gods.

The waters of Connla's Well rose up in fury all around her, boiling and bubbling and overflowing from the banks. They carried her body away from that place in a torrent, running south over the green land. Sionnan knew nothing more, as the water filled her lungs. Her skin was pallid and her skilful fingers were wrinkled as the water deposited her body in a shallow, hundreds of miles downstream in the new river that still bears her name.

As the clear waters played with her flowing dark hair and kissed her lifeless skin, Sionnan's body began to dissolve, and all her wisdom and skill and longing and energy dissolved into the water with it.

That is how Sionnan became the river, and the river became her.

THE RIVER DAUGHTERS

The peak of Pumlumon is the highest point in mid-Wales at 2,467 feet. This mountain is the source of the rivers Severn, Wye and Rheidol (a tributary of the Ystwyth that meets the sea at Aberystwyth).

The Romanised version of Hafren is Sabrina, and the river was first recorded in the second century. Many stories have been told about the origin of the rivers Severn and Sabrina, although it's difficult to know how many came from the imagination of Geoffrey of Monmouth! It is certainly a mighty river. By the time it reaches the sea, the Severn has the second biggest tidal range in the world, and the phenomenon of the Severn Bore at the highest tides, when a wave travels rapidly upstream against the flow of the river.

This little story, originally from Bill Gwilliam, plays on the origin of these three rivers mentioned in a lot of old folklore texts. It has some similarities to the story of Tamara, Tavy and Torridge. I like its description of landscape.

When the world was young, the giant Pumlumon met in the middle of Wales with his three daughters. They were grown up now, and eager to explore the world. They talked for a long time about the best routes to take and the things they wanted to learn.

The first daughter, an impatient girl, was direct. 'I want to travel to the salt water and the wild places beyond, and I want to get there as quickly as possible.' She faced west and became the River Rheidol.

The second daughter was more contemplative. 'I want to take my time travelling,' she said. 'I want to see the most beautiful places, and follow the curve of the land around

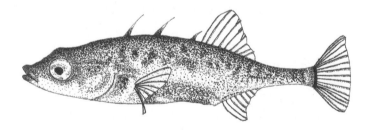

great woodlands and mysteries of the earth.' She faced south-east and became the River Wye.

The third daughter, though, was inquisitive. 'I am curious about these people that walk the land, and where they settle,' she said. 'I want to hear their chatter, know their sorrows and joys, and be part of their towns and cities as they grow.' She faced east, and she became Hafren, the mighty River Severn.

The giant watched as the waters of his three river daughters glistened and chattered through the land, each on their own journey, each to eventually meet again as their water diffused through the great ocean that surrounded the islands of Britain.

He sighed, and smiled, and he continues to watch to this day.

2

RUNNING DEEP

… the old heron from the lonely lake
Starts slow and flaps its melancholy wing …
John Clare (1793–1864)

As part of the great cycle of water, rivers become the arteries of the landscape – bringing water and life – and veins – draining away water and whatever else comes off the land. But in some places, rainwater is slow to drain away and the water is lethargic.

Where the land is low lying, surface or ground water creates wetlands: fens, bogs and mires. Sphagnum mosses retain water and create the layers of soaked, semi-rotten vegetation that eventually turn into peat. Still pools and lakes form in depressions in the ground, fed by rainwater or springs. Other still waters are dug for water supply, or they are created from quarrying or altering river flow. These places are all part of the freshwater systems of our islands.

In our traditions and our folklore, still waters throughout Britain and Ireland are home to monsters and wonders, dark secrets and surprises. Here's a selection of very different traditional tales about these diverse, wonderful watery places in our landscape.

DOZMARY POOL

Dozmary Pool, on Bodmin Moor in Cornwall, is one of the sources of the River Fowey. It is a Site of Special Scientific Interest, and the Fowey valley forms part of the Cornwall Area of Outstanding Natural Beauty.

Folklore insists that Dozmary Pool is bottomless, and that a tunnel connects it to the sea, ten miles away. Dozmary is one of the lakes laying claim to the last resting place of Excalibur, the legendary sword of King Arthur that Bedivere threw back to the Lady of the Lake after the Last Battle (perhaps at nearby Slaughterbridge). The folklorist Sabine Baring-Gould associated this place with 'witches' ladders', a type of enchantment binding feathers to a rope, each feather representing a spell or a curse.

There's no doubt that Dozmary Pool is a bleak place when the wind whips across the moor and the rain lashes down. This story has everything: howling gales, justice, devils, Christianity, witchcraft and good old-fashioned comeuppance.

If you ever find yourself staying on Bodmin Moor, and you are safe and snug indoors of an evening, be very thankful for the bar across the door and the light of the fire. For in the dark, no matter the time of year, the wind will howl as it sweeps up through the valley and on to the bleak moor, and the bogs will be calling for fresh blood as the rain drives against the windows.

But if the howling winds turn into a scream of terror, be sure to think no more of it, in case a restless spirit attaches himself to you. It's only old John Tregeagle, doomed never to stop, in case he falls into even greater torment: a hell that he already knows all too well.

In life, John Tregeagle came from an old and well-respected family; he was a steward in the service of the local lord. He oversaw the work of the peasants, whose lives were hard, working the meagre land through the seasons.

John Tregeagle was a cruel master. His heart was as hard as the granite of Bodmin Moor. Many peasants unfairly lost their jobs and even their lives at a word from Tregeagle, and many widows and children had reason to curse him.

But Tregeagle had power. Everyone knew that if you challenged him, you would be the loser. So nobody did. Tregeagle's pockets were filled to overflowing with gold from his ill-gotten gains, and he enjoyed his comforts.

There was only one thing that didn't grudgingly show John Tregeagle respect, one thing that never shows any of us respect – and that was time. John Tregeagle's body wrinkled and stooped and creaked, and then he died. Was anybody sorry?

A new steward was appointed. On his first day at work, he went over the lord's accounts, and noticed that one farmer hadn't paid his rent to John Tregeagle.

When the new steward demanded the rent, the farmer was outraged. 'I've paid it already!' he cried.

'Why did Tregeagle not record it then? All his other records are immaculate,' replied the steward.

Now the farmer was in a proper fix. There was no proof that he had paid (for who would dare to ask John Tregeagle for a receipt?) and he had no more money to pay it again. He faced jail, or worse. It seemed that John Tregeagle was to have one last victim.

The farmer went to see the local parson on the moor, to ask for help. This parson was a good man with a reputation for helping the poor; some said that he was a cunning man.

The parson listened carefully to the farmer's trouble, and thought deeply.

'How strong is your faith in the Lord?' he asked. 'Is that faith strong enough to carry you through any ordeal, any difficulty?'

The farmer wasn't expecting this. He was talking to a parson, about matters of spirit, and so he had to think carefully about the honest answer, for God would be his witness. But this was the kind of question that nobody usually ever asked.

'In truth, sir,' said the farmer, turning his hat nervously, 'no, I don't think my faith really is that strong.' His face was bright red at the confession of it.

'Then I won't be able to help you, my friend. I'm sorry,' said the parson. The farmer squelched his way home across the moor in misery, his last hope of help all spent.

The days went by, and the date of the farmer's trial grew near as he turned the matter over and over in his mind. He kept returning to the curious question the parson had asked him. Just how strong was his faith? What was faith, anyway? Did faith get stronger, the more scared a person was?

The farmer was surprised to find that the closer his trial got, the stronger and angrier he felt. This situation was not fair on him; he had not done anything wrong, as God was his witness; and he believed that the truth would see him through. If truth and God were one ... Why, his faith must be strong after all!

The morning of the farmer's trial day dawned fair, and bright and early he was walking back up the track and banging on the parson's door.

'Try me,' said the farmer to a very surprised parson. 'Put my faith to the test. It's as strong as any man's faith. I've been wronged, and God will see me right.'

'I'll see what I can do, then,' said the parson. 'Go and stand over there, and don't move until I tell you it's safe to do so.'

The parson washed his hands with hemp-soap. He lit a piece of charcoal and threw some herbs on to it, filling the room with smoke. Then he took a stick of elder wood and drew a circle on the floor in front of both of them, muttering as he went.

Suddenly he stood tall, pointed the stick at the centre of the circle and shouted out: 'John Tregeagle! John Tregeagle! Come HERE. NOW.'

Like a bad mist over the moor, the crooked shape of the hated old steward formed in the air inside the magic circle. There was a whiff of sulphur, and dozens of little demons appeared around the outside of the circle, cackling and snorting and waiting to drag Tregeagle back to the infernal pits of Hell. The farmer stood stock still in terror; all he could do was watch.

'John Tregeagle. Did this farmer pay his rent?' demanded the parson.

A ghostly eyebrow was raised. 'Yes ... yes he did,' came the wheedling voice of Tregeagle from the shape in the circle.

'Will you swear the same in the court this afternoon?'

'Yes ... yes, I will,' said Tregeagle.

'Good. Keep your word, or suffer the consequences,' said the parson. 'We'll see you there, and I'm binding you to the world of the living in the meantime.'

Later, in the courtroom, the poor farmer stood in the dock as the charges were read out against him. He stated clearly that he had already paid his rent.

'Can you produce proof of your payment?' asked the judge.

'Nothing, apart from the word of ... John Tregeagle,' replied the farmer, his voice wavering. The whole courtroom roared with laughter, but it stopped dead as the dark ghostly form of John Tregeagle appeared in the witness box.

'Order! ORDER!' cried the judge. 'This is most unusual, but let the witness have his say.'

The first and the last in that courtroom heard the familiar wheedling voice of John Tregeagle give his evidence.

The judge, part scared, part relieved and a tiny part very impressed indeed, declared that the farmer was free to go; and hat in hand, our farmer walked from the courtroom to hearty cheers from all sides.

But the ghost stayed in the witness box and it wouldn't go away.

The judge looked at the ghost very pointedly indeed, and the ghost looked at the judge rather sheepishly, if a ghost can look that way; neither of them knew what to say next. Then there was a commotion outside, and a white-faced usher hurried into the courtroom.

'M ... m'lud, there's a problem outside,' he stuttered.

'Yes, yes, what is it?'

'Er ... demons, m'lud. Little demons. Lots of little demons, making all manner of noise, m'lud. They say they want John Tregeagle back in Hell. Some nastiness about fire and brimstone. Horrible smell out there, too.'

Now the judge had a quandary on his hands. Here in front of him was the spirit of a wicked man that had been temporarily released from Hell. But the wicked man had now done a good deed (possibly the first good deed he had ever done) by telling the truth and saving an innocent man from punishment. Did Tregeagle deserve to be forgiven now? Was it right for good Christian people to send him back to Hell? And was it correct for the judge to try and play God and make the decision?

It was a most interesting afternoon, if a little chilly.

For hours and hours, they debated the issue in the courtroom, while the ghost of John Tregeagle watched the proceedings miserably and the demons howled and cackled around the outside of the courthouse and rattled the windows in a very annoying fashion.

At last, someone suggested that as the parson had raised the spirit, he should decide what to do with it now. The parson, in his cunning wisdom, made a suggestion that he hoped would satisfy all sides.

'Tregeagle should remain in the earthly realm, but he should be kept busy with a task from which he can never rest, to make sure that he doesn't lapse back into his wicked ways,' said the parson. 'If he strays from that task, even for a moment, then the demons will be permitted to take him back to Hell immediately.'

The judge was pleased, and relieved. Now the burning question became: what should John Tregeagle's task be?

It was agreed. The parson spirited Tregeagle's ghost to a north Cornwall beach. Tregeagle had to sweep out the sand from the caves and the dunes back to the sea. As he neared completion of the task, the sea swept the sand back again: it was a hopeless task that never ended. And so Tregeagle was set to work.

But one night in a great storm, the exhausted ghost dared to stop for just a second, hoping the demons wouldn't notice. There was no chance of that. The little imps were there immediately, cackling and snivelling and taunting him with flame. Tregeagle's ghost ran, and the demons chased him: past the dunes, through the woods and up to the bleak expanse of Bodmin Moor. The wretched ghost tried to get in at the window of a little chapel at Roche for protection, but only his head got inside before the demons were on him, clawing at his backside, and the ghost screamed in terror.

A young priest had been praying inside the chapel, and now he couldn't think straight for the howls of pain coming from the ghost, and the chatter and cackle of the demons outside. This was beyond the priest's abilities to solve, and so he called for the bishop. With great ceremony, solemn face and pointy hat, with book, bell and candle, the bishop bound the spirit of the unhappy ghost and spirited it away again: this time to Dozmary Pool on Bodmin Moor.

The ghost's task was now to empty Dozmary Pool, using only a limpet shell that had a hole in it. Tregeagle worked night and day at this impossible task, protected from the demons who were still baying for his blood.

John Tregeagle is working there still, howling with anguish and pain at his impossible task, all across the bleak bogs and pools of Bodmin Moor.

Now you know his story, be sure to lock the door at night.

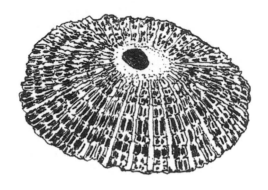

THE LADY OF THE LAKE

At an altitude of 1,660 feet, Llyn y Fan Fach is a lonely lake to the north-west of the Brecon Beacons in Carmarthenshire. It nestles in the hollow beneath sharply rising mountains, close to the source of the River Usk, in a landscape that has been managed by farmers for centuries.

The Physicians of Myddfai mentioned at the end of this story appear in the historical records of the thirteenth and fourteenth centuries. There has been a great deal of recent interest in their reported remedies and legacy, including benefits for the tourist industry.

However, much of the land around Myddfai and Llyn y Fan Fach is managed in a very different way now compared to the old days. In common with many of Britain's uplands, long-term over-grazing with modern breeds of sheep has led to wide expanses of species-poor grassland with very few heathers or herbs, and barely a tree for miles; peatlands are eroding and the potential for the land to hold carbon or water is diminished.

We can do better than this, for nature and for ourselves. In recent times, the conservation and re-wilding movements have been attempting to bring diversity back to the uplands, including the Brecon Beacons, and perhaps it won't be long before it is possible to find many of the herbs used by the Physicians of Myddfai in the landscape where they reputedly worked. The recent breeding success of the once-scarce red kite is an inspiration for positive change.

High up in the gentle hills of the Brecon Beacons, in a bleak, lonely place, there is a broad lake, called Llyn y Fan Fach. Around the lake, the turf is close cropped by sheep and there are few trees for miles. There is little sound, save for the high-pitched screams of the red kites as they soar overhead. But underneath the surface of that lake is another world.

Many years ago, a widow lived nearby with her only son, Gwyn. As he grew up, he was sent to mind the black cattle as they grazed the land around. Best of all, the cattle liked to graze around the edges of Llyn y Fan Fach, where the sedges, willows and sweet gale flourished.

One day Gwyn was walking along the edge of the lake with the cattle when he looked out to the water and started. There, walking across the surface of the lake as if it were clear dark glass, was the most beautiful young woman that Gwyn had ever seen. She was clothed in green, and smoothing her long dark hair with a golden comb, using the surface of the lake as a looking glass. Her face was glowing and clear.

Gwyn gazed on her full of wonder, and she suddenly sensed that she was being watched and looked up. He held out the only thing he had to offer: barley bread and cheese that he had been given for his lunch.

The lady walked across the surface of the water towards him, looked at his hard-baked bread and gravely shook her head.

'It's not that easy to catch me,' she said, and she slid under the surface of the water.

Gwyn went home, full of wonder at what he had seen, and sorrow that the lady had gone away. He told his mother everything and they pondered over the lady's refusal of the bread. Perhaps it was the fact it had been hard-baked? Gwyn's mother made bread dough that evening, and he packed some for the morning.

The following day Gwyn was awake well before dawn, and his mind was full of thoughts of the lady in green. By the time the sun was rising, Gwyn was already by the lake, watching and waiting as the blue sky and the gleaming sun reflected off the water's surface.

Gwyn waited all day, hour after hour, but he saw nothing but ripples as the wind ruffled the water's surface, and the odd silver fish flipping momentarily out of the water. He heard nothing but the sound of the cattle grazing contentedly at the water's edge.

By late afternoon, in despair, he was about to return home when the lady appeared out of the water again – even more beautiful than he had remembered. He had prepared all kinds of fine words to say, but nerves held his words, and all he managed to do was hold out the bread dough as an offering to her.

She looked at the dough with a solemn face and shook her head.

'I will not have this.'

Then she smiled at him, a smile so knowing and gracious that he was dazzled – and she disappeared.

Gwyn walked home slowly, warmed by the smile and the encounter, but wondering what on earth he could bring the lady as an offering she might accept. At home that evening, he asked his mother for advice.

'As the lady has not accepted hard-baked bread and has not accepted unbaked bread – why not take bread to her that has only been half-baked?' said his mother. So half-baked bread was made in preparation for the morning.

Gwyn didn't sleep much at all that night. Well before dawn the next morning, he was out of the house and walking down towards the lake, half-baked bread in his hand.

The sun rose, the clouds came across and rain fell heavy on the land and the water, but nothing could stop Gwyn's eyes from searching the surface of the lake that day, waiting and waiting for the lady to appear. The cold of the evening time had already started him shivering, and he was about to leave in disappointment, when across the water's surface there walked … not the lady, but six fine black cows.

As Gwyn watched, the lady again emerged from the water, following the cows. She slowly walked over the surface towards the land. In a trance, he walked into the lake to meet her, holding out the half-baked bread in his hand, heart beating fast.

Smiling, the lady took the bread, and allowed him to lead her on to the lakeside. As her feet touched the soil, Gwyn noticed that she was wearing leather sandals, and the sandal on one foot was tied in a different way to the other. She smiled again, and now Gwyn found his voice.

'Lady, I wish you to stay here with me. Lady, if you would consider marrying me, I would be the luckiest man alive.'

Her head began to shake slowly, but he pleaded with such passion that eventually she agreed. 'I will only marry you on two conditions,' she said, slowly. 'One, that you never tell anyone that I come from the lake. Two, that you will not strike me any blow without a cause. If you strike me three times without a cause, I will return to the lake and leave you forever, no matter what the circumstance.'

'Lady, I could never strike you, or break your confidence in me,' he began, but now she had turned from him and walked back into the water again! He was distraught now and crying, wondering what he had said wrong, and bemoaning his bad luck to the waters of the lake, when a voice behind him called out.

'Come here, lad.'

It was a tall, stern man in green, his hair and beard all wild, and either side of him stood a maiden with long dark hair. Gwyn approached him nervously.

'You wish to marry one of my daughters? So, tell me which one you love, and I will release her to you.'

Gwyn looked in the face of each of the maidens, and it seemed to him that both of them were the lady from the lake; he could not tell any difference. Terrified of choosing wrongly, he looked from one to the other and back again, and back again, until one of them put her foot forward, and Gwyn looked down. This lady's sandal was laced differently on one foot than the other!

'This is the lady I love,' said Gwyn.

'You've made the right choice,' said the old man, 'and I know you will be a kind and loving husband for her. I will give her as a dowry as many cattle, sheep, pigs, goats and horses as she can count of each without drawing another breath. And remember, if you strike her three times without cause, she will return to the lake.'

Gwyn was overjoyed. The lady stepped forward and her father invited her to count the number of cattle she wished to have, and she counted in fives until a single breath was spent: instantly, forty fine black cattle emerged from the water of the lake. The same thing happened for sheep, pigs, goats and horses, and Gwyn found himself in the middle of a braying, bleating, lowing menagerie. Somewhere in the middle of all the noise, the old man disappeared; and Gwyn took his lady's hand and led a noisy procession back to his mother's house.

The wedding was held in great celebration, and Gwyn and the Lady of the Lake – whose name was Nelferch – set up home in a farmhouse at Esgair Llaethdy, near to Myydfai, where they lived very happily for many years. Three fine sons were born, and they grew up amid plenty with the farmland, the hills and the lakes beyond to play in. Nobody ever found out about Nelferch's origins, and they didn't need to know.

When their eldest son was seven years old, Gwyn and Nelferch travelled to a wedding in the next village. They had barely ridden a mile when she stopped.

'I've forgotten my gloves,' she said. 'They're on the kitchen table.'

'I'll go back to get them,' said Gwyn.

By the time he returned with the gloves, he found Nelferch waiting in exactly the same spot, looking into the distance as if she was in a trance.

'Come on, my love, back to the real world!' he joked, and flicked her with the gloves.

She turned to him and her face was sad. 'That was the first causeless blow,' she said, and reminded him of the condition on which she was married, which he had almost forgotten.

Gwyn was horrified, for he had meant no harm, and he resolved to be more careful in future.

Many years later, they were at a christening, where all the guests were full of joy and hope and laughter. In the middle of it all, Gwyn found his wife sobbing.

'Whatever is the matter?' cried Gwyn.

'I'm crying,' she said, 'because I can see this child's future, and her life will be short and weak and full of pain.'

Gwyn tapped her impatiently on the shoulder. 'Should we not be joyful for the gift of life in whatever form it takes?' he asked.

'And that was the second causeless blow, husband,' she said through her tears. 'Be careful my love, lest you lose me forever.'

After this, Gwyn was careful every single day, in case he made another careless mistake that he might regret. He knew that if he lost the love of his life, and the wonderful life he had with her, that it would break his heart and the children's hearts as well.

Sometime afterwards, the little girl whose christening they had attended died, after a short life full of illness and pain. Gwyn and Nelferch went to the funeral, and while all around were mourning and full of sorrow, Nelferch threw back her head and she started to laugh.

Gwyn, embarrassed, took her a little too roughly by the arm and led her to one side of the room. 'Wife, what are you doing? Why are you laughing?'

'I'm laughing,' she said, wiping her eyes, 'because the poor child is at last free from suffering and in a happier place. But that was the third causeless blow. I will leave you now. Farewell.'

She left the funeral then, heading for home, and Gwyn followed, distraught. 'Nelferch! Come back! I didn't mean anything by it!'

At the farmhouse, she called her cattle to her, all by name, then the sheep, then the pigs, then the horses, then the goats. To each one she said, 'Come home. Come home.'

The animals followed her in a trance, and even the little calf that had recently been slaughtered jumped off the meat hook in the pantry and followed the lady away from the farmhouse, towards the lake. As they walked through cotton grass and asphodel and heath, she continued to call, and all the stock in the fields joined her, too, in silent procession following the Lady of the Lake. Last of all came Gwyn, unable to do anything about it.

Nelferch arrived at the edge of the lake, and silently walked into the water that closed above her head. The animals followed, until the only sound was the wind rippling the water of the lake and the call of kites above.

Gwyn was broken-hearted. He tried to follow them into the lake himself, and he was only saved by his three sons, who pulled him from the water and persuaded him back to the farmhouse. It was then that Gwyn told his three sons about where their mother had come from, and to where she had returned.

In the days and weeks that followed, father and all three sons wandered the land every day, from sun up until sun down, looking out to the lake and hoping against hope that their beloved wife and mother would return.

One day, the three boys were gazing out over the lake and sharing their memories, when their mother appeared, all robed in green, and walking over the water as if it were dark, solid glass.

'I will not stay,' she said, 'but I have a challenge for you. Do not just stay in this place, and keep its wonders from others. Explore the land, learn about the plants here, those that harm and those that heal. You have a great deal to give, to heal suffering and to cure the ills of people. Go and make a difference in the world.'

Inspired by their mother's words, the three lads studied hard, and walked the land with new eyes. They collected betony, nettle and cleavers, and they roamed far and wide to find they herbs they needed. They became skilled botanists and learned as much as they could about herb craft, physiology and healing.

The Physicians of Myddfai, and the descendants of Gwyn and Nelferch, became the most skilled doctors in all of Wales.

Mire Mischief

Bogs can be dangerous … very dangerous. Here are three cautionary tales for travellers. The first is from my local patch of Dartmoor, and it's a story I hear quite frequently, so perhaps it could be true! The second was collected by folklorist Ruth Tongue; and the third is an old Welsh fairy tale.

A man was walking on the high moor one day when he realised he was on a track next to bright green ground. He looked closer around him, and saw whorls of sphagnum moss, tiny sundews waiting for their prey, yellow spikes of asphodel and clumped white cotton grass waving in the breeze.

He tested the bog with his foot and it quaked and rippled.

'Probably best to stay on the path,' thought the man.

Up ahead, he also saw a hat lying on the bog. He picked up the hat, and underneath the hat was a man's head.

'Are you all right?' asked the first man.

'Yes, I'm fine,' said the second man. 'But in truth, I'm not so sure about my horse.'

∾

They say that Exmoor ponies can climb a cleave, carry a drunk and see a pixy. And that's just what old Farmer Mole's pony did.

Farmer Mole wasn't like a mole at all; moles are small, furry, agreeable creatures. No, Farmer Mole was a drunken old toad, and he gave his poor wife and children a shocking life of it. He only came back from market when his pockets were empty, and he'd be so full up with cider that he'd roll off his pony and sleep the night in the ditch. If Farmer Mole's wife hadn't stayed up waiting for him, though, he'd beat her good and proper, and do the same to the children, too.

The pixies didn't like this, and they decided to change things. They knew they could trust the old pony; he was foot-sure and wise, and he'd put up with Farmer Mole for years.

One foggy night the farmer was wicked drunk and swearing his head off, riding down the track to home, when he saw a light up ahead. 'Home already,' roared Farmer Mole, trying to stop the pony and nearly falling off again. 'I'll tan her hide for lighting a candle, I'm not made of money!'

But the pony wouldn't stop. He could see the pixy holding up a light, and it knew that over there was the blackest, deepest bog on the moor – it would eat up a pony in a moment, rider and all, if it were allowed.

'Hoi, FOOL of a pony, we're HOME, stop!' shouted Farmer Mole, punching and slapping about the pony's head. The pony took no notice. It rode straight towards the bog, and then it planted its little feet in the ground and stopped all of a sudden. The farmer fell to the ground with a crack to the head, but he was determined.

He walked forward towards the light, two steps, four steps, six steps.

The bog took him and swallowed him up whole, and then there was silence.

The pony trotted home, and when Farmer Mole's wife and children saw him back at the farmhouse, with peat muck all over his legs but with no rider, they lit every candle in the house and they *danced*.

After that fateful night, Mrs Mole left a pail of clean water out every night for the pixy folk to wash in, and she swept the hearth clean for the pixies to dance on.

They all prospered wonderfully, and that old pony grew as fat as a contented pig.

∞

A young harper near Bala was asked to travel to Ysbyty Ifan to play at a wedding party. The day went well, and he played well and long into the night, but when the evening was done, he had nowhere to stay. 'It's well into springtime, and the good weather is with us,' he thought. 'I'll be fine in the dark, I may as well set off for home now.'

As the harper walked across the hills he only had the light of the moon to travel by, and that was quite romantic. But the path soon disappeared as a thick mist descended all around him. He could barely see past his own feet now, and he held faith in the well-trodden track as far as he could see it, but when the ground became very sodden and springy underfoot with moss, he soon realised that he and the path had parted company.

One more step forward, and his foot couldn't find solid ground at all. It sank into the mire. His weight was on that foot, so he couldn't regain his balance, and the poor harper found himself sinking into a thick, soupy bog that seemed to have no bottom to it. He yelled and grasped on to tufts of rushes, but they came away in his hands. He tried to use his harp as a life raft on the surface of the mire, but he only lost his beloved instrument as he himself sank lower and lower.

The bog drew the harper down until only his head was above the surface, and then he gasped for air and made the effort of a final, desperate scream for help. The cry died away in the thick night mist, and all was hopeless.

Then the fog cleared suddenly, and by the light of the moon the harper could make out the shape of a little man at the edge of the mire.

The little man threw him a stout rope, and the harper struggled to fasten it under his arms. Then the little man pulled, and pulled, with the strength of someone four times his size. Gradually, with much squelching and oozing, he drew the harper out of the mire and he stepped on to solid ground, tired and thankful.

'Come with me,' said the little man. He led the harper along a little track into the middle of the mountainside itself. There were lights blazing and music playing and little people dancing. The harper was given clean linen clothes to wear, and a big goblet of honey mead to revive his spirits.

Then a little lady came forward, the most beautiful lady the harper had ever seen. 'Dance with me,' she said, and he did. They danced all night long, and the only regret in the back of the harper's mind was that he had left his beloved harp behind in the stinking mire. When the whole company retired late, the harper was given a bed of soft goose feather down, with the lady next to him, and he thought he was in very heaven.

The following morning, the harper thought at first that he was waking to a kiss from the lady; but he opened his eyes and realised a shepherd's dog was licking his cheek. He rolled over on the rough heather and grass of the mountainside, and then he sat up, rubbing his eyes, completely bewildered.

There was the big, treacherous bog stretching out below him. He was lying in the grass and heather next to the rough wall of a sheepfold, with no trace of a doorway to the place where he danced the night before. His clothes were covered in mud and peat, and lying next to him, plastered in the same stuff, was his harp.

3

ENCHANTED WATER

Come away, O human child!
To the waters and the wild
With a faery, hand in hand,
For the world's more full of weeping than you can
understand.

W.B. Yeats (1865–1939)

Rivers are a barrier, a division between one place and the next, and in the old days they were often dangerous to cross. River boundaries appear a great deal in myth and folklore around the world – think of the River Styx that divided the living from the underworld of the dead in the Greek myths. The boundary is often guarded by magical creatures or enchantments.

Not surprisingly, British and Irish folk tales are full of mischievous little people hanging around rivers, always ready to cause trouble for humankind. Some of them might even help out, if they want to: but beware, because they decide the rules.

JAN COO/THE PIXY AT OCKERRY

If you are out and about in the West Country, the mist descends on the land and you happen to see 'them' – you know, the fairy folk, the Little People, the piskies – then watch out, for you are in mortal danger of being pixy-led. Crossing the boundary between the human world and the magical realm may sound very alluring, but all the reports suggest that pixy mischief will lead to you getting lost, dazed and confused, and sometimes all three. There are some remedies: turn your coat or your pockets inside out, or find some clear running water to drink. At least water might help to stave off any hangover that's waiting in the wings!

This curious little story is about the Dart, a beautiful river that lends its name to Dartmoor in Devon. The River Dart can be fast flowing and dangerous on certain reaches, although these days the rapid waters are enjoyed for whitewater kayaking and canoeing.

Sadly, the old saying about the River Dart at the end of this story still seems to hold true, even in modern times.

Below Sharp Tor, but above the steep, oak-clad slopes of the River Dart, there is a farm called Rowbrook. Centuries ago a young lad looked after the cattle here. He was out on the land in all weathers, never saying much, just doing his job to the satisfaction of the farmer.

One winter evening the lad turned up at the farmhouse, all excited and quite out of character.

'Someone's calling for help, down at the river! There's trouble – we need to go and see.'

It was past the dimpsey time, and it would soon be pitch black outside, but the farmer and the other labourers went to the point above the river-slopes and listened. The river rushed and gurgled beneath them, but they could hear no voice.

'It was there! Loud as anything, I swear it,' said the lad. Then out of the darkness, as if it had heard, a plaintive, stringy little voice piped up.

'Jan Coo! Jan Coo!'

'What's wrong? Can we help you?' shouted the old farmer. But there was no reply.

Lights were fetched, and the men searched the woods all the way down to the river, calling out, and scrambling and stumbling across the rocks. Nobody was found; and so they trudged back up to the farmhouse, cold and damp, not knowing what to think. They searched the whole area again in daylight, but could find no sign of anyone or anything untoward.

That evening, the farm workers were warming themselves by the fire after a hard day's work when the lad rushed in again. 'The voice is back! The same voice!'

With some grumbles, the men went out into the pitch black again to the same spot at the top of the slope. There was the insistent little voice again: 'Jan Coo! Jan Coo. Jan COO.'

The farmer shouted out again. 'Do you need help?'

But there was no reply. Perplexed, the men went back to the warm farmhouse and the welcoming fire.

'I'll wager it's the piskies playing tricks,' said the old farmer as he settled back in his chair by the fire. 'They can make themselves sound like humans, when they want to.'

'Well in that case, we should pay no heed no matter how many times we hear it,' said the farmer's wife sternly, and that was that.

And heard again it was. That little wheedling voice called out every night after that, should anyone have cared to listen, and always saying the same thing: 'Jan Coo! Jan Coo.'

The winter rolled on, and there was a point when it seemed endless; but then the little daffodils poked their heads up from the ground and the catkins dangled from every hazel branch.

One evening, as the sun was low in the west, the young lad was climbing the wooded slope from the river, talking to one of the farm labourers. They were both looking forward to their supper.

Then the voice came again, this time from the other side of the river. 'Jan Coo! JAN COO!'

The lad answered in reply, but used the same words in mimicry: 'Jan Coo!'

The voice replied this time, louder and more urgent than before. 'JAN COO!'

'You go on to the farm. I'll go and see what it is, and join you in a bit,' muttered the lad. 'I've never been happy about that voice.'

Before the other could make him stay, the lad ran down the hill towards the river, jumping from boulder to rock to tree stump, towards one of the rocky crossing points in the river. All the time the voice was calling urgently, like an owl repeating its song, 'Jan Coo! Jan Coo!'

His companion watched as long as the light would allow, and then made his way back to the farmhouse for his dinner, hearing the voice calling behind him all the time. When he got to the farmhouse door, he lifted the latch, and listened for the voice once again – but it had stopped. There was nothing but the noise of the rushing river below.

He went into the farmhouse then and told everyone the story.

They were jumpy that evening, eating their dinner, and fretful afterwards by the fire. Hour after hour went by, but there was no sign of the lad. They went out into the pitch dark and called to him; they took lights and searched the wooded slopes the best they could; they went to the river, but the lad had vanished.

They never heard the little voice again after that, and they never saw that farm lad again. Everyone knew that he had been taken by the piskies.

Sometimes, if you listen very carefully to the sound of the river as it burbles and seethes its way from the moor to the sea, you can hear the sound of human voices.

River Dart, River Dart,
Every year you claim a heart.

೦ల

Humans are not always held captive by the fairy folk – sometimes it's the other way around. This rather satisfying little tale happened further upstream near Princetown on the Blackabrook, before it flows into the West Dart and the main river.

It's a harsh life, living on the high moor, and it's a good idea to be home before nightfall.

One evening, a woman was making her way across the moorland path to Beardown, and her step quickened as the light faded and the mist rose from the mires. She saw the bridge over the Blackabrook ahead, and knew there was some distance yet to walk.

When she was a few paces closer to the bridge, she saw a little figure walk out from the mire and up on to the bridge.

It wasn't as tall as a deer. It was only about eighteen inches tall.

It didn't have a big tail like an otter.

It didn't move like a fox. It was cavorting and dancing on two legs, not walking on four.

It had to be a pixy.

The woman stopped in her tracks. What to do? She couldn't turn around and find another way, there wasn't enough light left. She had to get home to her family, but she knew she now ran the risk of being pixy-led.

This woman was stout-hearted, and she resolved to press on. Just to be safe, though, she turned her shawl inside out, pulled out the lining of her pockets and drew up all the courage she had inside of her, before she carried on walking to the bridge.

Her footsteps squelched in the moorland mud.

Squelch.

Squelch.

The pixy was chuckling to himself, jumping from side to side on the bridge and doing some quite impressive acrobatics. As the woman approached it didn't stop, but skipped towards her, blocking her way, its sharp little eyes twinkling in the dimpsey light.

Without thinking much about it, she grabbed the pixy around its little waist, popped him into her basket and secured the cover. 'There!' she muttered. 'I won't be pixy-led. Let's turn the tables, shall we? I'll lead the pixy.'

There was a moment of perplexed silence, but only a moment.

Even though it was a large basket, there wasn't much room in it for a pixy of that size, so it was forced to lie still. But that didn't stop it chattering. A flow of pixy words now streamed from the basket, in a language she couldn't understand.

'Oh really? How interesting,' she said, striding over the bridge with the basket on her arm.

The voice chattered and burbled and nattered away.

'I'm so glad you made that point,' she said, 'very interesting. Tell me more.'

The pixy words continued, and by pretending to have a conversation, the woman kept her wits about her as she walked.

After a little while the little voice stopped. Was it bored, she wondered? Had it run out of words? Was it asleep? Or was it trying to trick her?

Now as she walked, she wanted to look in the basket to see what was going on.

She cautiously lifted up the cover of the basket by an inch or so, and peeped inside.

The basket was empty.

THE WHITE TROUT

This story was collected by the wonderfully named Samuel Lover in the 1830s, and picked up by W.B. Yeats in his search for Irish folk tales. It comes from a little village called Cong that straddles the border between County Mayo and County Galway. Cong is on an island surrounded by streams, and the short River Cong flows into Lough Corrib.

Back in the ancient days, a beautiful lady lived in a castle next to the great lake, and she was betrothed to a king's son. The years ahead were full of promise until a jealous courtier murdered the prince and threw him into the lake.

The poor lady went out of her mind, crying constantly, and refusing her food, until one day she disappeared from sight. Nobody knew where she had gone, and they said the fairies had taken her.

In time, a strange story began to spread at court: there was a white trout in the River Cong that ran to the lake. More and more people saw the fish, gleaming in the sunlight on the days when Mayo was blessed with fine weather. But nobody ever dared to try and fish it out, for they said it was a fairy fish. It was seen for years and years, a flash of white in the water, until the oldest in the village said that it had always been there, and everyone felt somehow safer for it.

The years turned, and war came again to Ireland, bringing hardship but also new people and new ideas. A bunch of soldiers came to the village, and one night in the bar they learned the story of the white trout, and they roared with laughter.

'Fairy fish? Now we've heard it all,' said the loudest and boldest of the soldiers. 'Now, if I were to cook and eat that fairy fish, I'd be the luckiest of them all, isn't that right?'

The next day that soldier went fishing, and sure enough he caught the white trout, for it wasn't difficult to spot. The soldier grinned. Away home with the gleaming fish he went, and he put it into a hot frying pan with fat sizzling.

The fish squealed and squealed, but the soldier just laughed – he laughed so hard you'd think that his sides would split – and he turned it over to cook the other side.

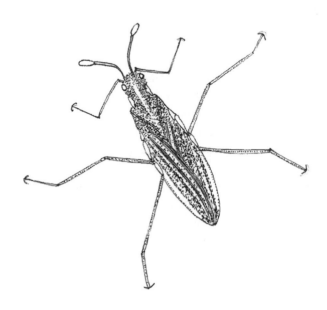

Strangely, the fish seemed untouched by the hot fat and uncooked.

'I'll give it another turn by-and-by,' he said, but when he did, the other side was no more cooked than the first. He knew he was in the wrong, but he kept cooking until he had run out of patience, with not a mark on the fish, and it squealed and squealed all the more.

'Well, my noisy little trout,' he said, 'perhaps you were done enough already; you might taste better than you look,' and he sliced a knife into the side of the fish to cut it for eating.

There was a murderous screech then, and the trout jumped out of the frying pan and on to the kitchen floor. It disappeared, and in its place stood a beautiful woman, dressed in white with a band of gold in her hair and a stream of bright scarlet blood running down her arm.

The lady was furious. 'You villain,' she shouted, 'look, look where you have cut me! Couldn't you leave me comfortable in the river, watching as I always do, and have some respect?'

That soldier whimpered like a puppy, and stammered and stuttered in front of the lady. He asked for her pardon, and begged for his life. Then his curiosity got the better of him.

'May I ask your Ladyship what you were watching for?' he asked.

'I was watching in the river for my true love, of course,' she said, 'and if he turns up while you have dragged me out here, I'll turn you into a little minnow, and I'll hunt you up and down the river for ever more, as long as grass grows and water runs.'

The soldier fell to his knees and begged for mercy.

'Renounce your villainous ways,' she said, 'and put me back into the river again, just where you found me.'

'Oh, my lady,' said the soldier, 'I would be a true villain if I thought I should drown you now.'

Before he could say another word, the lady in white disappeared, and there was the little white trout on the ground. The soldier put her on to a clean plate and ran down to the river.

As soon as that white fish touched the river water it ran as red as blood, for a day and a night, until the river washed the stain away; and to this day there is a little red mark on the side of every trout, where the cut was made.

Some say that the white trout still swims in that river, watching and waiting. But from that day forward, the soldier was a different man, and he went out of his way to create kindnesses wherever he could. In church he always prayed for the soul of the white trout; and you can be sure that he never ate fish again.

MUCKETY MEG

Here's another story that warns us not to mess with the fairy folk. It was collected by folklorist Ruth Tongue from an old lady in Lancashire in 1939. 'Go away and roll in the muck like Muckety Meg' was a common retort to a grubby child in the North Country.

In the old days, rivers and wells were often the only direct source of clean water, and so perhaps they were valued more as a result.

Gowan is an old Northern word for a yellow or white meadow flower, such as daisy, buttercup or dandelion.

Young Meg was very poor, but very pretty. Her rosy cheeks shone out from behind the dirt and her blonde curls fell prettily around her face when she scraped her long tresses up on her head.

Meg's family worked on a farm, but she thought that she was above such things. 'I'm so pretty, I'm sure that something wonderful will happen for me,' she thought. So she twinkled at all the lads in the village, and she gave herself airs and graces, and she wouldn't do any of the dirty jobs around the farm.

In truth Meg was a lazy lass, and she never bothered to sweep or dust or clean herself either. She was sure that her good looks would see her through. Above all, Meg wouldn't go near the animals on the farm. She wouldn't ever mind the sheep or brush down the horses or, heaven forbid, muck out the cowshed.

Meg walked past the sheep and stuck her nose in the air at their matted behinds and burry fleeces. The sheep answered 'Dirty beast!' but she didn't understand them: all she heard was baas.

She refused to milk the cows, and tiptoed round the cowpats with disgust. The cows answered 'Mucky Minny!' but she didn't understand them: all she heard was mooing.

She wouldn't go near the pigsty because she said that pigs stank, and when the pigs answered 'Filthy girl!' she didn't understand them either: all she heard was grunts and squeals.

One spring morning Meg was walking up on the hill when she should have been helping out on the farm. There, under the trees at the top, was a bower, all woven with leaves and flowers. It was swathed about with bright silks and satins, pinks and purples and blues, and there in the bower was the most beautiful gown Meg had ever seen, all of golden cloth.

Meg put on the fine golden gown over her old rags and grubby skin and greasy hair, and she moved the skirt this way and that in the sunlight, and she pranced and danced and curtsied as if she were a fine lady.

But Meg should have been more careful. It was a fairy bower. When the fairy folk saw her prancing about on their land, wearing their fine clothes, and making them all grubby with her dirt, they decided to teach her a lesson.

A voice sang out from behind the trees:

Muckety Meg she wears a fine gown,
She stole it, she stole it from Down a Down,
She never paid a filthy penny,
And why? Because she hasn't any.

Meg found herself glued to the ground on the hilltop, and her feet wouldn't move. She looked down at her fine golden gown and she saw, to her horror, that it was covered in muck. A lot of muck. The skirt was smeared in cow pats, the bodice was all over pig filth, and the fine trimmings were daintily dotted with sheep droppings.

Even though she couldn't see them, the fairy folk were in full voice now. They were singing, and laughing, and making such a racket that the sheep and the pigs on the hill all crowded round to see Meg, and they bleated and lowed and laughed and laughed. Then the animals joined in the chorus:

Nobody likes a grimy lass,
Nobody wants a stinking girl,
Nobody needs a dirty beast,
Go away and roll in the muck.

But Meg couldn't even do that – she couldn't move from the spot. All she could do was stand there and be laughed at, and she didn't know where to look.

People from the valley below started to walk up now, wondering what all the noise was about. Soon there was a crowd of people all around Meg, yelling and hollering and singing:

Nobody likes a grimy lass,
Nobody wants a stinking girl,
Nobody needs a dirty beast,
Go away and roll in the muck.

Then Meg saw a rather fine gentleman standing at the front of the crowd, all dressed in green velvet. She called out to him in desperation: 'Will you not help a pretty lass?'

'Yes, I can help you,' he said, 'but you must pay with your two blue eyes.'

'But what will I see with then?' she wailed.

'Green eyes,' he said, and he took away Meg's blue eyes and replaced them with green ones. Those eyes wept big tears, and the tears rolled down Meg's face and made streaks in the muck.

She called to the gentleman in green again. 'I'll give you my fine golden gown if you set me free.'

'That gown is not yours to give, because you stole it,' he said. 'I want real gold. There's all your pretty golden hair under that dirt, so I'll have that.' He stepped forward with silver shears and cut all Meg's golden hair off, so that she was left with short curls close to her head. Meg screamed and cried all the more.

'Now, go and wash in the river,' said the gentleman in green.

Meg found that her feet could move again. She pushed through the jeering crowd and ran as fast as she could, down the hill to the babbling brook in the valley, and she jumped straight in, golden gown, rags and all. The river water rushed around her and scoured the muck from her skin. She stayed in the river for a good while, and found that she actually quite enjoyed it.

Then Meg climbed out of the river, and there was nobody about: the crowd had gone. She looked down at her hands, and they were bright and clean. She looked down at her dress, and the golden gown had disappeared; but her rags were dry and neat and clean as a gowan.

A pig walked past. 'Good morning, clean lass,' he said.

Then a sheep came by. 'Pretty hair, curly clean locks,' she said.

Then a cow walked past. 'Come up to the Fairy Knowe,' she said, 'and I'll let you milk me, my pretty clean lass.'

So Meg walked up to the fairy knowe again. She took a silver pail and a milking stool from the fairy bower and milked the cow. The cow waited patiently, and afterwards said that Meg hadn't done a bad job at all.

Meg looked about her. Now the fairy bower had disappeared, and when she looked back, the cow, the milking stool and the pail of milk had disappeared as well. All that was left was Meg standing on the hilltop, her short blonde curls framing her rosy cheeks, and her skin and her dress all scrubbed spotless and neat.

The sun shone down on her and warmed her clean face and clean hands.

'I'd best be out of here,' said the no-longer-muckety-Meg. She walked down the hill and back towards the farm, and there on the track was a young farmer walking in the sunshine. He had curly hair and rosy cheeks and a big grin.

'Good morning, my pretty lass. I'm new here, will you show me around?'

'That I will, gladly. You'll need stout boots for the farm,' said Meg, and she smiled at him.

THE STARS IN THE SKY

This is my version of a nonsense nursery tale first written down by Joseph Jacobs in 1890. It has quite a different character to many of the other tales in this book, having little sense and no real purpose whatsoever. I love the way this tale evokes the sense of wonder present at all stages of a river, from its source to the wide ocean. Enjoy the daftness of this story, and imagine both the sun and the stars twinkling in the water.

Once upon a time, and it wasn't in your time and it wasn't in your time and it wasn't in anyone else's time, but it was a very good time, there was a girl who cried all day and cried all night. Nothing was ever good enough for her, and all she wanted to play with were the stars in the sky themselves.

One fine day in springtime she set off to find the stars in the sky. She walked and she walked until she came to a little spring, bubbling out of the ground and soaking the land around.

'Good day to you, bubbling water,' she said.

'It is that,' said the little spring.

'I'm looking for the stars in the sky to play with,' said the girl, 'have you seen any?'

'Oh, yes,' said the little spring. 'As soon as my water bubbles up, the stars shine in it and give me their blessing. Wash your face in the water, and perhaps you'll find them.'

The girl washed her face in the cold water bubbling up out of the little spring, but not a star did she see. So she thanked the spring, and she followed the trickle of water from the spring until she came to a little stream.

'Good day to you, little stream,' she said.

'It is that,' babbled the stream.

'I'm looking for the stars in the sky to play with,' said the girl, 'have you seen any?'

'Oh, yes,' said the stream. 'The stars in the sky sparkle in my water and they make the little sticklebacks laugh. Paddle about, and perhaps you'll find them.'

The girl took off her shoes and paddled about in the little stream, but she didn't see a single star. So she thanked the stream, and walked alongside it until the stream became a river. Beside the river there was a broad water meadow, all full of flowers, and there she met the Little People.

'Good day to you, Little People,' she said.

'It is that,' said the nearest Little Person.

'I'm looking for the stars in the sky to play with,' said the girl, 'have you seen any?'

'Oh, yes,' said the Little Person. 'The stars shine on the grass and the flowers here at night. Dance with us, and perhaps you'll find them.'

The girl danced and danced to the merry pipes of the Little People until she was fair exhausted, but she didn't see a single star.

So she sat down in a heap on the grass and the flowers, and she started to cry.

'It's hopeless,' she said. 'I've washed and I've paddled and I've danced, but I couldn't find any stars, and unless you help me I shall never be able to play with the stars in the sky.'

The Little People whispered to each other, and one of them came up to her and took her by the hand and said, 'Dry your eyes. Here's what you have to do.'

The girl brightened up.

'Go forward, go forward, and mind you take the right road,' said the Little Person. 'Ask Four Feet to carry you to Two Feet, and ask Two Feet to carry you to No Feet At All, and tell No Feet At All to carry you to the Stairs without Steps. If you can, climb the Stairs without Steps.'

'Oh, are the stars in the sky really there, and can I be with them?' asked the girl.

'If you're not there, then you'll be somewhere else,' said the Little People, and they bowed to her and began to dance again.

The girl left the water meadow with a curtsey (remembering not to thank the Little People, for they don't like it), and she skipped alongside the river with a light heart until the water curved around and she met the woods. The big old alder trees whispered with their leaves and she got stuck in the mud several times, but she battled on through until the ground became easier to walk on again and the river was rocky and fast.

She didn't walk much further before she came to a huge, wizened old hawthorn tree, and underneath the tree was a white horse with a wild mane.

'Good day to you, white horse,' she said.

'It is that,' said the horse.

'I'm looking for the stars in the sky to play with,' said the girl. 'Can you carry me there? I'm so tired.'

'Nay,' said the horse, 'I don't know anything about stars in the sky. I'll only do something if the Little People tell me it's good to do.'

'They sent me here! They told me to tell Four Feet to carry me to Two Feet.'

'Well, why didn't you say in the first place?' said the horse. 'Jump up, and I will carry you.'

So they rode and they rode and they rode, always with the water in view, until the river was wide and tranquil and reed beds lined the edges, rustling in the breeze. They turned a corner and up ahead was the muddy place where the river widened out completely and met the sea.

'Get you down, now,' said the horse. 'I can't go any further, because there is no more land. I've done as much as Four Feet can do, and I must away home to my family.'

'But where is Two Feet?' asked the girl.

'I don't know,' said the horse with a flick of his white mane, 'and it's none of my business either. Goodbye!' and he was away.

The girl stood at the edge of the water where the river widened out to the sea, and she listened to the call of the birds. There wasn't much water to be seen, as the tide was out, just a wide expanse of mud. As the girl looked out across the mud, there was a loud peeping call, and a great bird flew down to the estuary and landed right in front of her.

It was black and white, with bright orange-red legs and a long, bright orange-red beak. It was an oystercatcher.

'Good day to you, oystercatcher,' said the girl.

'It is that,' said the oystercatcher.

'I'm looking for the stars in the sky to play with,' said the girl. 'Can you carry me there? I'm so tired.'

'That's outrageous!' peeped the oystercatcher. 'I don't know anything about stars in the sky. I'll only do something if the Little People tell me it's good to do.'

'They sent me here! They told me that Two Feet would take me to No Feet At All.'

'Well, why didn't you say in the first place?' cried the oystercatcher. 'Jump up, and I will carry you across the mud.'

The girl jumped up on the back of the oystercatcher and grabbed on to its feathers as best she could, as the bird determinedly put one webbed foot in front of the other, slowly, steadily walking across the glooping mud towards the sea. Other birds whirled around them and searched the mud with their long beaks for food, and a couple of them looked quizzically at their friend the oystercatcher; but none of them came close.

Finally, the oystercatcher stopped before a great expanse of salt water and waves that stretched as far as the eye could see. About halfway to the horizon was a wide glistening path running straight out towards a rainbow arc that rose out of the water and went up into the sky. The arc was made of all the colours in the world, red and yellow and green and blue, and it was wonderful to look at.

The girl put her feet on to the mud and stood next to the oystercatcher, staring at the wonderful sight. 'But where is No Feet, and where is the stair without steps?' she asked.

'I don't know,' cried the oystercatcher, 'and it's none of my business either. Goodbye!' and he spread his wings and flew back to the mud, peeping loudly as he went.

The girl looked back to the sea. There was a bothering of the water in front of her, and a big golden fish came swimming up.

'Good day to you, big fish,' she said.

'It is that,' said the fish.

'Can you show me the way to the stars in the sky,' said the girl, 'up the Stairs with no Steps?'

'Nope,' said the fish, 'not unless you bring word from the Little People.'

'Ah,' she said. 'The Little People told me that No Feet At All would take me to the Stairs without Steps.'

'Ah, that's good then,' said the fish. 'Get on to my back and hold tight – there, to the top fin – not to the side ones.'

Splash! Off he went into the water, with the girl on his back holding on for dear life, along the silver path in the water towards the arch. The colours of the arch glowed brighter and brighter the closer they got, so bright that the girl could scarcely look at it.

When they finally got to the foot of the arc, she saw a broad road sloping away into the sky, and at the end of the arc there were bright white lights dancing about. Were they the stars in the sky?

'Now,' said the fish, 'here we are, and you need to climb – but hold on fast, for it was never meant for your kind of feet.'

Off he went into the waves, darting golden into the deep blue.

So the girl began to climb, but she never got a step higher than when she started. She climbed and she climbed, but there was no foothold. She called out to the stars dancing ahead of her, and desperately tried to cling on to the rainbow arc, but her hands went straight through it. She was dizzy from the bright light, and numb with the cold, and at last she couldn't help but let go completely and sink down, down, down into the deep blue sea.

And crash! She clattered on to a hard floor and a tattered rug, and the girl found herself lying by the bedside at home, all alone in the dark.

4

CURIOUS CREATURES

Wise men of old said that everything on earth had its double in the water.

Charles Kingsley, from The Water Babies, *1863*

If you have ever taken a kick sample from a river or been on a pond-dipping expedition, you will know something of the wild variety of creatures that live in our freshwaters, usually unseen. Like its larger cousin the ocean, the watery world of rivers and pools is hidden beneath the surface, a complete mystery to most people for most of the time.

This other world can be alluring when the sunlight is shining, but malevolent and devouring if it's dark. What better place for all the monsters of our imagination to live? Dragons, worms, horses, mer-people, boggarts and unimaginably horrible beasts are all here, if you are brave enough to look, or unlucky enough to discover they've been your neighbour all the time.

Here are a few folk tales about the mythical fauna in the freshwaters of Britain and Ireland. Sometimes we learn about their appetites and their victims, and they brook no argument. Sometimes we are lucky, and they meet the unlikeliest of heroes.

WATER HORSES

Celtic mythology is full of water monsters who take the shape of horses, although some can be shape-shifters. The ubiquitous each-usige, *or water horse, has other counterparts: the nuggle in Shetland, the tangie in Orkney, the Welsh* ceffyl dŵr *and the Manx* cabbyl-ushtey. *All live in lochs, lakes and pools.*

Kelpies are a special kind of dark water horse spirit living in Scottish rivers, preying on humans where they can get them. Kelpie hooves are reversed compared to those of normal horses and they sometimes have a mane made of writhing snakes. If you come across a kelpie you are advised not to touch it, for you will stick fast; the kelpie will run down to the river to devour you, and then leave your entrails on the bank. You have been warned.

The River Conon begins at Loch Luichart in the Scottish Highlands and flows through Easter Ross to the Cromarty Firth. It is part of a large hydroelectric scheme ongoing in the Highlands since the 1940s, but the river is still considered good for salmon and sea trout.

The Conon is a bonny river, full of trout and eels and big pearl mussels. It's not one of those wild desolate streams in the uplands, nor does it rush and thunder with force across the broken rocks. Yet the River Conon holds more fear than any other river in Scotland.

You can hardly go half a mile along the Conon without stumbling over the scene of a horrible legend with the water-wraith or the kelpie. One of the most frightening of these places is Conon Woods. Over a swamp of yellow flag, with the corncrake screeching all around, there is a hillock covered in old willow trees, rising like an island from the mist with thick mirk-woods on either side. The river whirls around an old burial ground there, with the broken ruins of an old kirk. Among the fallen stones, you can still make out the archway of the main window and the little trough that once held holy water.

Many centuries before now, when that chapel was whole, there was a corn field on the land where the woods are thickest now, on the kirk side of the River Conon. One day in late summer, a group of Highlanders were busy cutting the corn and heaping it up, when they heard a voice from the river.

'The hour but not the man has come.'

They looked around, and there was a dark kelpie-horse standing in the river, next to the pool and the ford across the river from the old kirk. The kelpie snorted and said again: 'The hour but not the man has come.'

Then it disappeared into the pool.

The group wondered what it could mean, but not for long. A man in hot haste came riding down to the river, making straight for the ford. Four of the stoutest men broke away from the harvest to warn him of the danger. They told him they had seen a kelpie, and urged him to take another road or stay with them a while; but he was determined.

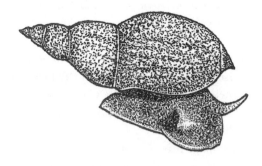

However, these were Highlanders and responsible men, so they took things into their own hands. They locked him up in the old kirk until midnight had passed, which is the fateful hour of the kelpie. In fact, they left him there all night, with refreshment to see him through.

The following morning the men came back to the old kirk, unlocked the door and flung it open. 'You can go in safety now!' shouted one Highlander to the traveller – but there was no answer.

There was the man, lying lifeless and cold on the floor, with his face deep in the water trough. The kelpie had come for him, locked door or no.

∽

Heisker, or the Monarch Isles, are a small, isolated group of islands about five miles west of Uist in the Outer Hebrides. About a hundred people used to live here in harsh conditions, although the islands have been uninhabited since the Second World War. Heisker is now a National Nature Reserve and a haven for sea birds and seals. On the main island is a ruined village surrounding Loch nam Buadh. Perhaps it is the same loch in this story, told in Gaelic by Donald MacDougall to his cousin Donald MacDonald in 1956.

On Heisker, fresh water was scarce in the summertime, and the women used to do their washing in the loch. The old men shook their heads. 'It'll be the worse for you, there's nothing to save us from the water horse,' they said, 'it will come for us all one day.'

And so, the village reared a fearsome bull that was never let outside, just in case one day they had to set it on the water horse. Meanwhile, the women would travel to the loch in pairs to do their washing, just for safety.

One day, and nobody knows why, a woman went to the loch on her own to wash clothes. She worked hard, and it was a fine summer evening by the time she'd finished, so she sat down with her back to a grassy knoll and dozed in the sunshine.

She didn't know how long she had been asleep, when the noise of footfall awakened her. There was a tall, handsome man smiling at her.

'Tiring work, washing, isn't it?' he said, by way of conversation.

'Yes, it is,' she replied. He had a clear face, high cheekbones, and flaring nostrils. She'd not seen him on the island before.

'I'm worn out myself,' he said. 'I've been walking all day. Would you mind if I shared this sunny spot with you?'

'Not at all, please do,' she said.

They sat next to each other in silence for a while, and it wasn't a disagreeable silence.

Then: 'I'm sleepy,' he said, 'would you mind if I laid my head in your lap?'

Well, this was unusual. Why not?

'I don't mind at all,' she said, and he did, and he fell fast asleep.

She couldn't doze; she was wide awake, and looked down at his sleeping head.

There was gravel from the loch on his scalp, and green water weed in his hair.

She looked at him more closely. He didn't have feet. He had hooves.

It must be the water horse! What on earth could she do, with him fast asleep like this?

She had a pair of scissors in her pocket, and so she cut out a circle of cloth from her coat, all around the sleeping head of the man, and then she moved slowly away from underneath and placed his head on the ground very carefully indeed.

She walked away for a few steps to be quiet, and then ran for her life. A mile up the road towards the village, she looked over her shoulder, and there was the water horse in its true form now, dark mane swirling, galloping like the wind after her.

So she shouted loud, she shouted for anyone who could hear, 'The bull! Release the bull! Release Tarbh na Leòid!'

The bull was let loose by the farmer, and it met the water horse with all its weight and might. The two huge animals laid into one another then, and they were an even match for a while, but then the bull started to push the water horse out towards the great sea beyond. Both animals disappeared under the waves and that was the last anyone saw of them.

The woman went to bed after that, but she never left it again.

Many years later, a great bull's horn washed up on shore in Heisker. It was put to good use, as a bar across a gateway.

THE LAMBTON WORM

The mighty River Wear rises in the Pennines and flows east through County Durham to meet the North Sea at Sunderland. It has a significant industrial history, with lead and coal mining and limestone quarrying, and the Wear still suffers from heavy metal mineral pollution as a result – although much has been done to restore the ecology of the river.

County Durham also has a rich cultural heritage, and this is one of the area's most famous folk tales and songs. Worm Hill, a small hill to the north of the Wear near to Lambton Castle, is known locally as the place where the Lambton Worm coiled its evil body at night.

In folklore, 'worm' is often used as another name for 'dragon', although of course there are many types of dragons.

Our landscape is full of stories of giant water worms, some mysterious and elusive (do you believe in the Loch Ness Monster?) and some much more destructive and hungry for flesh, human or otherwise.

Some think that the Lambton Worm was a lamprey: an ancient, eel-like fish that have toothed sucker mouths instead of jaws. Lampreys have always been a prized food, considered a luxury for the nobility. One old name for lamprey is 'nine-eyed eel' as lampreys have seven gill slits, a nostril and an eye on each side of their heads. There are three species of lamprey in British and Irish rivers: the river lamprey and sea lamprey are migratory, while the smaller brook lamprey stays in freshwater for its whole life cycle. Sea lampreys can reach up to a metre long, but nothing of Lambton Worm proportions!

The first written reference to the Lambton Worm is in William Hutchinson's 1785 notes on the folklore of County Durham. He suggested that the story may be an allegory for the terrors of Viking invasion. The tale has been adapted by several writers including Bram Stoker. I was fascinated to learn that Anthony Shaffer, the screenwriter for 1973's classic film The Wicker Man, *wrote another adventure for Sergeant Howie called 'The Loathsome Lambton Worm' – but it was never made into a film.*

Working with the story now, I find myself pondering a different perspective: what would happen to any of us if we fished our darker sides out of the river and took no responsibility for them afterwards?

'Kye' is the Middle English and Scots word for cow.

John Lambton was the only son of the local lord, and he was a wild young man. He listened to nobody and he cared for nothing, except himself. In particular, he took great delight in not going to church on a Sunday with the rest of the village, and going fishing instead on the fast-flowing

River Wear. Once a week at their worship, the whole of the congregation had to endure his ripe, creative curses from the river bank outside: some about themselves, and some about the lack of good fishing.

One Sunday morning, John was out fishing and his curses were louder than usual. It was a sunny, clear day, and the trees and flowers by the river were out for full summer; but there were no salmon to be had, no roach or dace. He had to wait for hours, but finally his line went under: something had bitten!

He pulled and pulled at the line, cursing all the time, and above the surface of the water a little head appeared.

It wasn't the head of a fish. Even from the river bank, John Lambton could see the creature's blinking, glittering eyes. Nevertheless, he got it in to land.

There, lying at his feet in the mud, was a small but revolting beast. It was about five inches long, mottled grey and slimy, with all the makings of a hideous worm.

John prodded it with his foot, and it wriggled.

He reached down and gingerly picked up the creature, and it lay docile in his open palm. He could see that it had nine holes on either side of its head, like the gills of a fish, but more primitive. As if it could read his mind, the worm opened its little jaws and clamped them on to his thumb.

'OW!' John dropped the thing then, and I couldn't tell you the filthy language he used.

'What's that you've caught there?'

John swung around and there was an old, old man with a wrinkled face and beetling eyebrows, standing a little too close behind him.

'I've got a devilish creature here,' said John. 'Do you know what it is?'

The old man just shook his head sadly.

'Ah, dear,' he said. 'It will do you and yours no good to

bring this out of the river – yet you cannot throw it back. You have found it, and you must keep it.'

With that, the old man shuffled off, still shaking his head.

John took the gruesome little creature and carefully put him in a pocket, thinking to scare somebody with it later in the day. But as the hours wore on, the stink of the thing, and the disagreeable wriggling and farting noises coming from his pocket, were so unsettling that John walked down to the well outside of Lambton Hall, his father's home. The creature was thrown into the well, deep down into the darkness and out of sight, and John waited for the delay before he heard a little 'splosh' as it hit the deep water.

'You won't cause any problems there,' said John Lambton.

A few years went by, and every day that worm down the well grew a little bit older and a little bit bigger, out of sight in the deep. What manner of dark food did it find there to feast on? None can tell.

One day, the worm finally got just too big for the well, and it slithered its way out, fully grown, many yards long and revolting. As soon as its stinking tail had cleared the well, it made its way to the River Wear and coiled itself around a rock in the middle of the river, close to Lambton Hall.

Every day the worm would stay there, fouling the water, and every night it would slither out of the river and make trouble in the countryside around. It drank the milk from cow's udders, bothered the horses, gobbled up the lambs and frightened anyone who had the misfortune to be nearby. Once it had had enough fun for the night, it would retire to a nearby hill about a mile from Lambton Hall, where it would coil itself three times around the hill and fall asleep. Its snores shook the land for miles.

John Lambton soon heard about the trouble and went to see for himself. There were the nine holes on each side of the grey slimy head; there were the glittering black eyes. This was his fault, and he felt a pang of shame for the first time in his life. Nobody must know it was his fault! Perhaps he should quietly get out of the way?

John took the vows of the Cross and went on a Crusade soon after that, hoping the creature would disappear while he was away. He left his old father on his own at Lambton Hall, with a promise to return with renown and a deal more wisdom.

That summer, the worm got bolder and bolder. Soon, every night it would cross the river and come right up to the hall. The old lord was wide-eyed at the windows of his great house, virtually a prisoner to the beast. He soon found that he had trouble not only from the hideous worm, but from the people who appeared in protest with pitchforks and scythes, demanding action.

The next day, the steward of the hall asked all the dairy maids to bring all their milk and fill a great trough in front of the stables. That night the worm swallowed all of the milk and then, without any further trouble, went up to the hill to sleep and coiled three times around the hill, snoring.

But the lord's worm management strategy didn't work for long.

After that the worm crossed the river every day for milk, and woe betide the people if the trough contained less than nine kye. The worm would hiss, its eyes would goggle, and it would lash its tail around trees in the park, uprooting them and using them as clubs. Soon the whole landscape was wrecked, with great craters in the soil and no other living animals in sight.

For seven long years the great worm terrorised the land around Lambton Hall. Scores of people and even more animals were lost to the dread beast, and the more it ate, the bigger it became. Brave knights came to destroy it, but they all suffered the same sorry fate; the monster slowly crushed the life out of anyone who came near, and then ate them all up, spitting armour from its teeth like so much tin foil.

One autumn afternoon, young John rode back down the track to Lambton Hall, returned from his adventures in the Crusades, towards the place of his birth. But the landscape of his youth was wrecked, and his lip trembled as he surveyed the ripped up parkland, the ravaged earth, with no sign of crops or animals. All the farms around the hall were deserted for terror of the great worm.

When he got to the hall, at least his father was still alive, and John Lambton managed to tell him the truth about how the worm was found.

'Well, son, it can't be helped,' said his father. 'But it's down to you to do something about it, and soon. Go to the wise woman in the next village, and ask her advice.'

The wise woman peered at John Lambton through the thick herb smoke from her fire.

'You and you alone can kill the worm, as you're the one who found it, young man. But there's only one way to kill it. Go to the smithy and have your armour covered in metal spikes and spear heads. Then, wearing the armour, go to the worm's rock in the middle of the river and stay there. When he comes back from the hill at dawn, you can fight the beast, and may luck be with you.'

'Thank you,' said John. 'I think I'll need luck.'

'Ah … talking of luck, there's one more thing,' said the old woman. 'If you do manage to kill the worm – and it won't be easy, mind – you must swear that you will also kill the first living thing you see afterwards as you cross the threshold of Lambton Hall. If you fail to do so, then none of your family will have the luxury of dying in their beds, for nine generations hence.'

'I swear,' said John Lambton.

He walked back to the hall in deep thought, then he put plans into action. He had spearheads welded to his armour all over the breastplate, back and arms and thighs.

John didn't worry his father with the vow he had made to the wise woman; but he arranged with servants at the hall that when they heard three notes from his hunting horn, they should release his favourite dog to meet him at the threshold. His dog would be sure to run and meet him, and although it would be sad to lose him, it was the best way of ensuring he wouldn't set eyes on anyone else first.

Then John put on the armour and walked, with difficulty, to the rock in the river where the worm lived in the daytime; and there he watched with tired eyes, sword drawn, until dawn.

Even so, he didn't hear the worm approach, slithering silently across the land in its accustomed trail and into the river water. It was only when the huge head reared up out of the river, and a glittering black eye fixed on him, that John Lambton saw the worm for the first time since he had thrown it into the well, all those years ago. But now the worm was huge, and he was tiny and vulnerable.

Did it recognise him? John didn't wait to find out; he had no intention of being bitten again. All his experience of bloody battle in the Crusades was put to good use now, as he slashed and parried with the head of the hideous beast. The worm darted across the water with surprising speed, jaws snapping this way and that, and the river rose up around it in turmoil.

John's fighting was impressive, but the worm was wily. As its head was dealing with the swordplay, its tail was slowly coiling around the rock in the river, up and up until it was coiling around the body of John Lambton. The brave fighter was so busy fending off the jaws of the monster that he didn't notice until it was too late: and then the worm tightened its coils and tried to crush him alive.

The jaws of the beast stopped snapping then. The harder it squeezed around John and his armour, the deeper the spear heads dug into its flesh. Soon the water was bright with the creature's foul, frothing blood, and its grip loosened.

As soon as he could break free, John used his sword to cut the worm in two. The creature shrieked and tried to attack again, but it had lost too much blood, and it rolled back into the River Wear to die.

After the worm had gurgled its last, a strange peace settled on the wreckage of the land, but John could not rest yet. He waded through the river towards Lambton Hall, and as he staggered up the hill across what used to be a field, he stopped, pulled his hunting horn from his belt, and blew three loud notes.

John was nearly at the hall now, nearly home, and he looked up as there was something running down the slope towards him; and then he froze. It wasn't his favourite dog running to meet him.

It was his father, old Lord Lambton.

'No,' muttered John. 'No, no, this is too much to ask of any man. I cannot kill my own father!'

He embraced his father and they walked back up to the hall to celebrate. John tried not to think about his vow, and told himself it was all just superstition. Nevertheless, the poor dog was put to death later that night.

The following morning, father and son set about the recovery that you rarely hear about in stories: putting the land to rights and repairing the great damage wrought by the Lambton Worm. John worked hard to restore the place, and for the rest of his life he was a devout, brave, community-minded man.

But the fact remained that John Lambton had broken his vow, and even though he never knew it, nine generations after that suffered the consequences. Whether they died in battle, were thrown from horses or drowned, Lambtons died violent, sudden and sometimes cruel deaths.

All of this happened because, one sunny day, John Lambton fished a strange, dark little creature out of the river.

THE MERMAID OF MARDEN

Here's a particularly English story from Herefordshire. You might recognise the river character, more usually found in salt water at the coast.

In the old days, the River Lugg used to be a lot closer to Marden church than it is now. One time the good people of the parish were getting the church bells out for a clean. Church bells are heavy, and it took many people to carry a single one. While they were carrying one of the finest bells back towards the church, someone stumbled, someone else lost their grip, and one of the bells fell in the river.

As it fell, everyone saw her. There was a young woman in the river, and she had green water weeds for hair, and a shining silver tail instead of legs. Everyone was sure she was a mermaid.

Whatever she was, she took the bell and dragged it underwater to the bottom of the river, and she wouldn't give it back no matter how nicely they asked. It was all a bit embarrassing, because church bells are heavy things, and the little slip of a mermaid seemed a lot stronger than they were.

How should they get the bell back from the mermaid? God was silent on this issue. The priest had to swallow his pride and go to see the village wise man.

The wise man's instructions were very precise. 'You'll need twelve white heifers, pure white, mind,' he said, 'twelve yokes carved of yew wood, and bands of rowan for all of them, or they'll end up in the river as well. Be sure to drag the bell out of the river in complete silence, just so's you don't wake her up.'

So they got the heifers and the yew wood and the rowan, and all very softly, softly they attached chains to the bell and tiptoed away. The heifers started to pull and the bell came out of the river as easy as anything.

They saw the mermaid was all curled up inside the bell, fast asleep. Then one of the local farmers, forgetting himself in his excitement, called out: 'In spite of all the mermaids in Hell, now we'll land Marden's bell!'

Well, that did it. The mermaid awoke and immediately slithered back into the river carrying the bell with her, snarling at the yew wood and the rowan.

Marden parish church never did get its bell back from the mermaid. It's still there to this day, lying at the bottom of the river, and ringing clear as a mermaid's voice.

Some say it echoes the bells of the church. Some say it taunts them.

THE KNUCKER DRAGON

In Sussex, a knuckerhole is a large, deep, spring-fed pond. The word 'knucker' comes from the Anglo-Saxon nicor, *meaning water monster – a word used in* Beowulf. *Folklore tells us that knuckerholes are bottomless pits, often home to fearsome monsters, the most famous of which lived at Lyminster. The unmarked grave slab of the hero monster-slayer can still be seen at Lyminster church along with a stained-glass window depicting this story. The knuckerhole itself isn't far away, thirty feet deep and deceptively calm.*

At Lyminster, long ago, there was a knucker dragon, the biggest and greediest of all his kind. He'd lived in the big pond for a good while, and he fitted well in there at first, seeing as the pond went down and down with no bottom to speak of. Then he started to grow, and bits of his loathsome scaly body rested all over the fields and around the village.

The dragon crunched up all the sheep and the cattle thereabouts, which was bad enough, more than anyone should put up with. But when he began to eat the villagers, licking them off the road like a toad licks flies off a river stone, well, something had to be done about it.

The Mayor of Arundel sent out a call for help. There were no princesses to marry in Lyminster for killing a dragon, like in the old days, but he offered a hefty reward: more than a year's wages it was, and still nobody offered to kill the wretched beast. Autumn was nearly through, and the villagers started to wonder whether they'd ever get to see Christmas.

Finally, a young lad from nearby Wick put up for it. His name was Jim Puttock, and he wasn't tall, and he wasn't big, and he wasn't strong: but he did have a gleam in his eye.

'How are you planning to kill the dragon?' asked the mayor, curious, because young Jim didn't look like much of a hero.

'I'll need some supplies,' said Jim. 'Let's see. A big iron pot, big as you can get. Flour, lots of it; milk, a few gallons; butter, as much as the dairy can give; currants, a half hundredweight; honey, as much as the bees in the orchard have made this year. Oh, and some firewood.'

The ironmonger made a huge iron pot for Jim that was so big it wouldn't even fit in a barn, and all the supplies were fetched, with the villagers grumbling and muttering. 'He's on the make!' they said. 'This is no dragon-killing kit he's asking for. He'll do a runner, you mark him.'

Jim built a big pile of firewood outside in a farmer's field, over the other side of the village from the dragon, and it took six grown men to lift that iron pot on to the top of it all.

Then, as all the supplies were being brought in, and the villagers all asked to tip them into the pot, Jim slipped away quietly and went to the wise woman's cottage at the edge of the village.

The wise woman chuckled heartily at Jim's request. 'Jim, you'll be using up all my supplies as well, but I reckon you're on to something,' she said. 'Here's a basket, now. Wormwood herb – lots of it – and wolfsbane, and mistletoe, in they go. Yew gogs nice and ripe – mind you're careful to wash your hands now – and here's a whole load of those little pointy mushrooms, and some of those red and white pixie toadstools as well. Yes. I reckon that'll do the job, Jim. Good luck. Mind how you go.'

Jim went back to the great pot and lit the fire underneath until it smouldered hot. Then he took a small tree trunk and stirred the ingredients round and round until they were all nicely mingled and cooking on the fire. In went the contents of the basket, he stirred again, and the scent of sweet pudding wafted through the village of Lyminster and past the nostrils of the sleeping dragon. Jim Puttock was making the biggest pudding that had ever been seen, before or since.

Once it cooled down a bit, the iron pot was

tipped on to its side with the help of the strongest men in the village, and the pudding fell on to a timber tug, steaming and sinking in the middle in a pleasing manner. It wobbled as it was drawn through the village with heavy horses, and all the villagers came out of their cottages or peered down from the windows as the giant pudding went past.

None of them dared to go beyond the bridge, though, because there was the head and body of the knucker dragon, lounging in the fields, its tail trailing in the great pool.

Jim Puttock walked over the bridge and called out to the dragon from a good few paces away. The horses dragged the pudding over the bridge and stood there nervously.

'Afternoon, dragon!'

The dragon looked at Jim through sleepy eyes. 'Afternoon, man,' it said. 'What's this you're bringing past? It smells good.'

'Why, it's a great sweet pudding,' shouted Jim.

'Pudding? What's that?'

'Just try it, my friend,' yelled Jim. 'You'll like it.'

There was a snap of huge jaws then, and in one gulp the great wobbly pudding, the horses and the cart were all gone. Jim only managed to avoid being eaten by hanging on to an old elm tree by the road.

He crept out from behind the tree, and the dragon was licking its lips. 'Mmmm. A little snack. Perhaps only a starter?' said the dragon hopefully. 'Is there another one?'

'I'll bring another to you later,' shouted Jim. "Bye!' Then he ran as fast as he could, back over the bridge and away.

The villagers didn't know what to make of this little scene, but soon they had trouble. The dragon was not happy. It started to moan, and groan, and thrash about that way and this, uprooting trees and making great craters in the ground; chimneys were flying off the houses in the village and the bridge had several great chunks taken out of it.

It was getting near dusk when the dragon calmed down a bit and Jim dared to go back over the bridge. There, lying in the road, was the poorliest looking dragon you ever saw. I hope that you've been lucky enough to know what it feels like to eat too much pudding – that might have been enough, but with the bad herbs and the mushrooms as well, the dragon's head was dizzy and he wasn't seeing straight.

The dragon looked up from the road with difficulty and he saw three Jim Puttocks in front of him, whirling round and round.

'Don't give me another one of them puddings,' mumbled the dragon. 'Something wrong with my guts. Collywobbles. Woozy.'

'Sorry to hear that,' shouted Jim. 'I've got something that'll make it all better, though.'

Jim Puttock then brought an axe from behind his back and cut the dragon's head clean away from its body.

That was the end of the knucker dragon, and how the villagers cheered! There was a big party, and all the people in the village danced on the dragon's body and called Jim Puttock a hero. Even the wise woman came out to join the celebrations.

Mind you, Jim never cooked pudding again, and everyone was very glad of it. Perhaps because of the lack of pudding, he lived to a ripe old age.

5

METAMORPHOSIS

And out again I curve and flow
To join the brimming river,
For men may come and men may go,
But I go on for ever.

From 'The Brook', Lord Tennyson (1809–92)

The natural world is full of changes from one state of being into another: chrysalis into butterfly, leaf into soil, sunlight into energy. Within these processes, water is one of the deciding factors. Water makes up most of our bodies and the bodies of other living things around us, and we could not live without it for very long.

This is reflected in our folk tales, where water is often a major part of magical transformation. Water creatures change as we interact with them, often becoming more than they originally appeared. The river changes us, flows through us, inspires us, and washes us clean to start again … whether in this life, or the next.

THE FISH OF GOLD

*Poplars are wonderful trees, with shivering, whispering leaves and a thirst for water. The true black poplar (*Populus nigra*)*

*is one of our rarest native trees, and it propagates itself along
old river sides that have not been managed or messed around
with – a rare commodity in our modern landscape. If you are
lucky enough to find a true black poplar, rather than a hybrid or
a Lombardy variety, look out for its leaning gait, thick fissured
trunk and bright crimson male catkins in the springtime.*

*As for fish with scales of gold, they are a thing of fairy tales,
at least here. Ruth Briggs notes that this story was collected
from Johnny Smith in Kendal in 1924; however, it has many
similarities to particular German and Russian fairy tales, and
may have derived from them. I love the motif of the golden fish.
What does it represent for you?*

Once upon a time a poor fisherman and his wife lived in a
bare little cottage near to a great river. They didn't have many
possessions, but they had each other, and it was a pleasant
place to try and eke out a meagre living.

One day the fisherman put his net out into the water and
when he hauled it in there was a flash of gold in the net. At
first he thought it was treasure, but when he looked more
closely he could see that it was a fish covered in scales of
bright gold, flashing and glinting in the sun.

'Let me go,' gasped the golden fish, 'please put me back in
the water.'

The fisherman looked at the golden fish and considered
a moment.

'If you put me back in the water,' said the fish, 'I will turn
your cottage into a grand palace, and there will be a magic
cloth on the table that will give you anything you want to eat.'

The fisherman considered again. 'Very well, I will put
you back,' he said, and carefully picked up the golden fish
to throw it back into the water. The fish stayed very still, and
in a quiet voice it said, 'Thank you. Mind you tell nobody
about my gift, or it will vanish instantly.'

The fisherman nodded and put the fish back into the river. With a flick of its tail it was gone from sight.

He trudged home, not expecting anything more to come of the encounter. But when he rounded the corner towards home, he could see a huge wooden-framed building with turrets and flags and grand gates, just in the place where his little cottage had been.

Here was his wife, hurrying towards him in a fine silk gown. 'Husband! I don't quite know how this happened, but it is wonderful!' she beamed. 'Come inside.'

The palace was even grander on the inside than the outside. She poured him a glass of good red wine from a flagon on what used to be the kitchen table, now made of marble and covered in a golden cloth. 'All I have to do is think about what I would like to eat, and it appears!' she said. 'Try it.'

The fisherman closed his eyes and imagined a great pie, all crumbling shortcrust pastry and venison and juniper berries, and no sooner had he thought about it than he could smell it. He opened his eyes, and there in front of him was the most enormous pie he had ever seen!

There wasn't much conversation for a while after that, but when eating had finished she said, 'You don't seem very surprised by all of this. Do you know how it happened?'

'Don't ask me that, please. Just enjoy it,' he said.

'But I have to know,' she insisted. 'How did all this palace – this cloth – this food – how did it happen?' She wheedled and pleaded and would not let the matter rest.

Several hours later, after quite a few glasses of wine, he gave in, and told her all about the golden fish.

As soon as he did, everything disappeared – the finery, the palace, the marble table, the golden cloth, the good wine and good food. He and his wife were left sitting on their rickety chairs at the old kitchen table of the cottage, with rumbling bellies.

The following morning, the same as most other mornings, the fisherman put his net out into the river again to see what he could catch. When he hauled the net back in, there was a glint of gold. It was the golden fish.

'Let me go,' gasped the golden fish. 'Please put me back in the water. I will turn your cottage into a grand palace, and there will be a magic cloth on the table that will give you anything you want to eat.'

'Very well, I will put you back again,' said the fisherman, and carefully picked up the golden fish to throw it back into the water. The fish stayed very still, and in a quiet voice it said, 'Thank you. Mind, tell nobody – nobody at all – about my gift, or it will vanish instantly.'

The fisherman nodded grimly, remembering the night before, and put the fish back into the river. With a flick of its tail it was gone from sight.

The fisherman walked back with a little spring of hopefulness in his step. When he rounded the corner towards home, he could again see the huge wooden-framed building with turrets and flags and grand gates, just in the place where his little cottage had been.

Here was his wife, hurrying towards him in a fine silk gown. 'Husband! You did it again, come and see!' she cried.

Same palace, same flagon of good wine, same golden cloth, same table, same food.

'Was it the golden fish again?' she asked.

He wouldn't answer, nor on the second time, nor on the third. But still she asked and asked, until he gave in.

'Yes, yes, it was the fish again, now are you satisfied?' he cried.

As soon as he did, everything disappeared again, food, palace and all. He and his wife were left sitting on their rickety chairs at the old kitchen table of the cottage.

They looked at one another and the fisherman pulled a face.

'Sorry,' said his wife.

The next day the fisherman put out his nets into the river again. 'If only the golden fish were there again, if only we had one more chance!' he thought.

When he hauled the net in, there was the golden fish once again. It lay still as he carefully picked it out of the net and placed it on his hand.

'Once is luck, twice is coincidence,' said the fish, 'but now you have fished me out for a third time, I can see there is no point resisting fate. Here is what you have to do. Take me home and divide me into three parts. Give one part to your wife to eat, one part to your mare to eat, and bury the other part near to the river bank.'

'What will that do?' asked the fisherman. But the fish spoke no more, and its eyes went glassy and still.

The fisherman carefully carried the golden fish home and he followed its instructions: the fish was divided into three. One part was given to his wife to eat, one part to his mare, and the other part was buried close to the river bank.

In time, his wife gave birth to a little boy with hair made of gold, and the mare gave birth to a foal with a golden mane. Down on the river bank where the third part of the golden fish had been buried, a graceful poplar tree had grown, with cracked bark and leaves that shook and shimmered golden in the autumn time.

The boy with the golden hair and the foal with the golden mane were close friends from the earliest days, and they had many adventures as they grew up in the bare little cottage by the great river.

But by the time the boy with the golden hair had turned eighteen, he wanted to see more of the world. 'Mother! Father! I want to go and seek my fortune,' he cried.

'Why go out into the world?' said his mother. 'Our fortune came to us here – in the shape of a golden fish. You must be patient.'

'I must explore the world now,' he insisted. 'I will be safe with the horse with the golden mane. Mind you look out for the poplar tree with golden leaves by the river. As long as the tree is well, then I will be well. If I die, the tree will die. If the tree starts to wilt, then pick a leaf, put it in your pocket and come to find me.'

∽

The young man with the golden hair set out that day, riding the horse with the golden mane. They travelled through woods and over rivers, across wild heaths and through tiny villages, until they came to the edge of a great forest and a crossroads.

They stopped at the crossroads and the boy scratched his golden head, gleaming and hot in the sun. 'Which way to go?' he wondered. He noticed a fine horse tethered to a large oak tree nearby.

'Psssst!' a voice whispered loudly from the trees above the path. 'Up here!'

He looked up and there was a young woman's face smiling down at him from a great oak.

'Nice hair,' she said.

'Er … thanks.'

The young woman swung herself over a large branch of the oak tree. 'I wouldn't hang around here with that hair if I were you. There's a band of robbers about, and they'll kill you for it.'

'What can I do? I can't help my hair,' he said.

'A couple of muddy puddles should sort you out. Come with me.' She jumped down on to the path and led the young man and his horse to a shallow pond in the woods, where they covered the boy and the horse with enough dirt and mud to cover the gleaming gold.

She laughed. 'Now you look just like the rest of us!' she said.

They fell to talking, and the young man with muddy hair had never met anyone so knowledgeable, or witty, or funny. They laughed and joked all day long; and from that point onwards, they were inseparable. They explored the woods and the towns about, they dodged the robbers, they taught each other woodcraft and they shared their dreams. It wasn't long before the young man and the young woman were wildly in love.

'Tell me about your mother and father,' he said, a few days later, both of them sitting in a tree.

'Ah. That's complicated, and I don't really want to say.' She hung her head and blushed.

'I will need to know,' he said, going a bit bashful himself, 'because I think I'd like to marry you, if you'll say yes.'

She smiled, a sad smile. 'Well … Actually I'm a princess,' she admitted. 'I prefer being in the woods and climbing trees to wearing a dress, if truth be told. My mother was always horrible to me, until my father banished her from the court; and my father now wants me to be the perfect, girly princess. But I come out to the woods when nobody's looking. Much more fun.'

He whistled. 'I don't suppose your father would allow the likes of me to marry his daughter, then,' he said sadly.

'Not a bit of it.' She grinned. 'It's not his decision to make – it's mine – and I say that I will marry you! Let's go and find a priest who will marry us, right now, today!'

That's how the two were married, and their woodland adventures continued in love and bliss, but they couldn't last that way.

༄

Early one morning, nestled in the crown of a great oak tree, she woke him up.

'Stay quiet. My father's guards are under this tree. They've come to find me,' she whispered. 'We have to give ourselves up now, and go to meet my father.'

The guards marched them through the woods and over a series of hills until there below them was a city next to another great river, and in the middle of the city was a fine palace with golden turrets gleaming in the sunlight.

'Home, I'm afraid,' the princess muttered to her husband.

At the palace, the king rushed out to greet his daughter as the stable boys came to take away the two horses.

'You're filthy from head to foot, daughter! Go and wash and change your clothes,' said the king. 'But who is this young man?' He gesticulated towards our hero with his foot.

'This is my new husband,' said the princess. There was a gasp from the court and the king's brow furrowed.

'I will not allow it. Throw him in the dungeons,' he told his guards, 'and wash your hands after you've done it. He's even more covered in dirt than you.'

The following morning, our young man was wallowing in the castle dungeon after a very uncomfortable night when along came the jailor, with his keys rattling.

'Seems like you're to be brought in front of the king,' said the jailor.

In the throne room of the palace, the young man saw the princess again – this time unrecognisable in a deep blue taffeta dress and fine jewels, and with red eyes. She burst into fresh tears at the sight of him.

'Oh, stop blubbing, girl,' said the king. 'Young man, there is a mystery I would like to solve. When your horse was cleaned in the stables, they found it has a mane of gold. How do you explain that? Did you steal it?'

'It was born at the same time as me. We are inseparable,' said the young man.

'Father I keep telling you,' said the princess, 'under that dirt, my love has golden hair as well!'

It's a great feeling to have a good bath after weeks of being in the woods, and I won't tell you how filthy the water was when our young man had finished bathing. His golden hair was combed and he was dressed in fine clothes and presented to the king.

The king gasped at the transformation, and after that he seemed to accept the marriage between his daughter and the young man. The dungeon was never mentioned again. Our young man was welcomed into the royal family of that place and treated like a prince; which, by fact, he was. The prince with the golden hair.

෧෨

Many happy months went by, but the longer he stayed in court, the more our hero realised there was a problem: the king's advisor was going out of his way to make life difficult for him. Whenever the prince looked, the king's advisor was narrowing his small eyes and scratching his wispy beard and glaring at him.

The mutterings of gossip began at court. 'They say the new prince is a coward.' 'Never achieved anything in his life.' 'Just because he has golden hair, doesn't mean he's good enough for the princess.'

In court one day, the king's advisor leapt to his feet and bowed with a flourish before the king.

'My lord,' he said, 'there is news of a great dog otter that has been seen again on the river after many months. They say the otter is a creature of omen, and of magic. I say that we should send the new prince to find it and prove himself.'

'Good idea,' roared the king, and clapped the advisor a little too heartily on the back. 'Let our golden boy seek this creature. I'm sure he will have no problems finding it.'

So the task was set, and the golden-haired prince rode his golden-maned horse through the woods and down to the river. It was late afternoon in late summer, and by the time they got to the river bank their hair was glittering in the sunlight and reflecting from the surface of the water.

They didn't have to wait for long. A little way further upstream, a sleek brown head popped up about the river's surface and saw the golden hair glinting in the sun. Like all animals, the otter was curious, and it came to investigate. Both prince and horse watched, transfixed, as the otter played acrobatics in the water in front of them, and then swam away again in pursuit of some fish or other.

They followed, carefully, quietly, for what seemed like many miles, always transfixed by the otter's movements. By the time it disappeared, the prince looked around and realised it was nearly dark, and they were in a woodland miles from home. Up ahead of them, next to the river in a cluster of rocks and stunted trees, was a little cottage.

As they approached, the door opened and out came a bent old woman.

'Now, what would you be doing out here in the wilds so late at night?' she said, and peered at the lad as he jumped down from his horse.

The firelight from the cottage flickered in the gold hair on his head and the gold mane of the horse. The old woman started in wonder, and then muttered, 'Yes, yes, good ... no time to lose. Now, my lad, come a little closer so I can see that wonderful hair of yours.'

She reached out and touched the hair with her fingers, and as she did, the skin of the prince and his horse both turned cold grey and they were rooted to the spot, turned into stone – all but the gold of their hair.

∽

The following morning, many miles away, the fisherman was down by the river when he noticed the leaves of the poplar tree were drooping and turning grey. He reached up and pulled a leaf from the tree and put it in his pocket.

'Something's wrong,' he said to his wife. 'I'll go to find out what's happened to our son.'

He saddled up the old mare and they rode away through the woods with his wife's blessing. Whenever the fisherman was unsure about the direction to travel, the leaf in his pocket would jump: once for yes, twice for no. He rode through the night until, as dawn broke, he found himself following a broad river and a woodland alongside. It wasn't long until he could make out the dull gleam of gold ahead.

The fisherman leapt off of the mare and tied her to a nearby tree, and then he crept through the woods until he reached the stone figures, their skin cold and grey in the morning light. Tears ran down his face, but the poplar leaf in his pocket was jumping up and down, and he took it out and laid it on his palm.

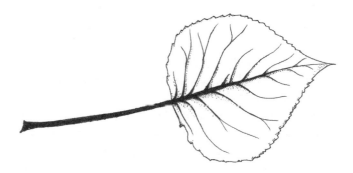

The poplar leaf had turned into pure gold. He touched the hair of the lad and the horse with the leaf, and the colour and life came back into them instantly. The horse shook its golden mane and the lad rubbed his eyes.

'Quick. Where is safety?' the fisherman asked.

The pointed leaf of the poplar tree turned like a compass to the west.

'Let's go!' He fetched the old mare, and the prince and his father rode away as the old woman, returning from a wood-gathering trip, howled with rage behind them.

∞

There was great celebration in the palace when the missing prince returned, together with his father.

'Never mind that silly old otter,' said the king in great good humour. 'We'll leave him on his own for now. It's more important you are safe, and the future of the kingdom is safe.'

In time, the fisherman and his wife both went to live in the palace – they had found their riches and their fine food and wine again, eventually. They took branches and twigs and leaves from the golden poplar tree and planted them by the river, and in no time at all the canopy of the woods was quaking and shivering and whispering, and golden yellow in autumn.

In time, the old king passed away, and the prince and princess became king and queen of that place, and ruled happily there for many years.

On the day after their coronation, the new king and queen wandered through the woods, sharing happy memories of the days when they had met among the trees, all those years ago. They came to the battered remains of a tumbledown little cottage beside a great river. And on a rock next to the river, something glinted gold.

The new king and queen looked closer. There were three pawprints in the mud next to the river, with round pads and rounded toes.

On the rock, as if it were a gift for them, was a small golden fish.

THE WOUNDED SWAN

Britain and Ireland have three species of swan. The mute swan, one of the largest flying birds in the world, is here all year round. The whooper and smaller Bewick's swans are winter visitors, and are said to herald icy conditions. Mute swans are the most common; our islands hold about half of all the mute swans in Europe.

During the twentieth century, many swans suffered from lead poisoning, but bird numbers have increased dramatically since anglers' lead weights were banned in 1987. I will never forget, several years ago, witnessing a Somerset stretch of the M5 motorway being held up by over a dozen swans who decided they wanted to sit on the road.

Once upon a time all swans in England were said to belong to the monarch and their favoured subjects on the 'swan roll'. Many unfortunate swans had their wings clipped or their beaks notched to denote ownership and make them easier to catch for the table. Roasted swan was a royal dish indeed, sometimes yielding up to 20lb of cooked meat per bird; but, by law, nobody was allowed to catch or shoot a swan without permission, no matter how hungry they were.

The graceful, regal swan also appears frequently in heraldry. The symbol of my own home county of Buckinghamshire is a swan with a gold coronet and chain around its neck, possibly referring to a mythical 'knight of the swan' somewhere in the county's history.

Our culture has a complicated relationship with swans. They can be considered as a good omen, with bad luck following anyone who kills them; but swans are often persecuted, too. Roald Dahl's harrowing short story 'The Swan' made a powerful impression on me as a child.

This dark little tale comes from the Cambridgeshire fens, long since drained.

On the fens in the old days, people often went hungry, and in the summer when the water was lower, there were only so many fish and waterfowl to go around. But there were some birds you didn't eat, no matter what – and they included the swans. In one part of the fen, seven huge swans would hold court day after day, paddling in the fen and swimming on the lazy river nearby. No other water fowl dared to try and land in that bit of the fen, for fear of the seven swans. If anyone even so much as tried to steal an egg they would get more trouble than it was worth.

People worried about those seven swans. They said it was bad luck to set eyes on them, let alone hear them flying over you. People would cross themselves if they lay awake at night and heard the beating of seven pairs of swans' wings through the air above them.

One year the crops failed and disease in the cattle was bad, so a lot of people were hungry. It wasn't a good time to be a water fowl on the fen that summer.

A young fowler lived on the edge of the fen, and he was a good shot. He knew how to get something for the pot if you asked, and he wasn't afraid of breaking the rules – he fancied himself a bit above the law, on account of his shooting skills. That summer, after no proper food for three whole days, the fowler decided that no rule was sacred and that he would take matters into his own hands.

Early the next morning, the fowler crept along the track through the fen, shielded from sight by the tall reeds in the ditch, and he spied the seven swans on the marsh beyond, feeding.

He raised his gun to his shoulder, took aim, and fired.

Six of the swans rose up in the air in a flurry, wings beating wildly, but the seventh could not fly: it had been shot through the wing.

'So far so good,' he thought, 'now I've got to get it out of there.' He leapt over the ditch, landing ankle deep in mud, and cursed. Then he scrabbled forward into the marsh with a huge cloth sack and tried to pick up the fighting, injured bird.

The other swans desc-ended on the fowler then, hissing and pecking and beating him with their huge wings. He would have died for sure, but he snatched his iron knife from his belt and bran-dished it at the birds. Instantly they recoiled, and he finally managed to pick up the injured bird, using the iron knife as a threat to calm it down. Then, bruised and breathless, he carried a heavy sack full of struggling swan all the way back to his cottage.

The swan stayed still on the kitchen floor, a cloud of white feathers on the flagstones, with one wing stained with blood. It was a beautiful creature, quiet and dignified and intelligent, and for a moment the fowler felt a little guilty for what he had done. The swan stayed quite still as he opened out the damaged wing to look at the wound.

Still, the fowler's belly was rumbling wildly and demanding attention. He had to find the quickest and easiest way to dispatch the bird so that he could pluck it and chop it and roast it and eat it. This amount of meat would last him for a week or more! The swan's neck was slender and definitely wring-able, but he didn't like the look of that sharp beak. He decided to go outside to fetch his axe.

When he returned, the swan had disappeared. In its place, standing on the flagstones and looking at him defiantly, was a pale young woman dressed in white, with long golden-yellow hair and dark eyes.

The fowler couldn't kill and eat a young woman. So he bound up her injured arm, and decided she would live with him and keep the house, and do all the things a wife might do. She had no say in the matter. He made sure that she never went beyond the four walls of his little cottage.

The swan maiden never spoke, she never struggled and she never agreed to what was asked of her, but he took her to his bed that night, all the same.

The first night, he woke in the dark to the sound of great wings beating outside. The other six swans had arrived outside the cottage, pecking and crashing against the doors and the windows, beating the roof and stamping on the ground outside.

The door was barred, and the swans couldn't get through the tiny windows of the cottage. So the fowler laughed, part in fear, part in defiance. 'Ha!' he called out through the noise. 'I haven't taken the king's swans after all, I've broken no law. I've taken a swan maiden instead, and you will never have her back.'

The young woman lay in the dark and listened to her siblings beat against the cottage walls, and she smiled to herself.

The fowler and the swan-woman lived together in that little cottage for seven days, and every night the six swans outside beat their wings against the walls.

After seven days, the arm of the swan maiden was healed. Over the scar, and all the way along her slender arms, feathers of pure, gleaming white were beginning to sprout.

'What's this?' he shouted. 'I'll have no fairy tricks in this house.' He began to beat her black and blue.

The swan maiden's neck became long and curved then, her nose hardening to a yellow beak with black around the eyes, and her long arms changed to great white wings. The fowler had a great swan in the cottage now, and it was angry. A swan is a much better fighter than a fowler. It nipped and pecked and smacked him about with its wings, forcing him towards the door, forcing him to open the door, and then to go outside into the yard, where the other six swans were waiting for him.

The seven swans beat their gleaming white wings, and they pushed and pecked the fowler towards the middle of the fen. His body was found there the next day, bloodied and broken, face down in the marsh mud, with the swans feeding peacefully nearby.

Nobody else, bird or human, ever dared to go there after that.

THE POOL AT THE WORLD'S END

Traditional stories about frogs turning into princes really do exist. Versions of this story pop up all over England and Scotland, with various repulsive forms for the creature at the pool or well, and various circumstances for the young woman.

I think that frogs get a bad rap in fairy tales. They are amazing creatures. Frogs can breathe through their skin, hibernate in the mud for a whole winter, and change their skin colour to blend in with their surroundings. That's quite aside from their miraculous transformation from frogspawn to tadpole to frog, that we all learn about in school.

The European beaver is an essential part of our wetland ecosystem, reintroduced to many areas in recent years thanks to a huge effort by conservationists. It's great to be able to talk about these amazing creatures after lobbying for their return in Scotland, and then seeing them back in the wild, both north and south of the border.

I have played with this story a little (as many storytellers do) after working through some classic fairy tale themes that didn't quite feel right, and working on the environmental aspects.

Once upon a time, and it wasn't in your time, and it wasn't in my time, and it wasn't in anyone else's time either, but it was a very good time, there was a young girl whose father had died, and her mother was all on her own. She was a strong mother, but she was a strict mother, and she worked very hard to keep bread on the table and a roof over their heads.

The girl was expected to work just as hard as her mother, if not harder. There was no play for her, only sweeping and washing and cleaning and cooking. Whenever she had finished her jobs for the day, her mother would always give her more work to do, and nothing she did was ever good enough.

As the girl grew up, her mother got more and more tired and more and more despairing. 'Ah me!' she would cry. 'If only I had never got married and never had a child! Imagine what a fine and free life I could be living now! Everything's awful, and nothing will ever be happy any more!' She worked harder and harder, and became harsher and harsher. Her poor daughter felt like it was all her fault.

Eventually, one morning the mother thought to get rid of her daughter altogether, so she gave her daughter a sieve. 'Here,' she said, 'take this sieve to the pool at the end of the world, and fill it full of water, and bring it back here for me, or there'll be trouble.'

The girl started off on her journey: yes, it sounded impossible, but who knew what magic she might find along the way?

She passed a bunch of girls in the next village, and one of them called out: 'Where do you think you're going in such a hurry?'

'I've got to find the pool at the end of the world. I need to collect water from the pool with this sieve, here.'

But they just laughed and jeered at her. 'Idiot!' they shouted.

She carried on walking.

She walked past a group of farm workers gossiping over their lunch. 'Hoi, handsome, where do you think you're off to?' one of the lads cried.

'I've got to find the pool at the end of the world. Do you know where it is?' she asked.

The lad spat out his cider. 'Fairy tales!' he taunted. 'Get back in the real world, airhead.'

The girl walked on for many days, snatching food and sleep where she could, until her feet were tired and her belly was rumbling.

One day she was lucky: she had walked past a baker's shop and they had given her half a loaf of bread. Not long after that, the girl walked past a bent old woman in a shawl, hobbling along the rough track with some difficulty.

'Hello,' said the girl. 'Can I help?'

'I'm not sure you can,' said the old woman. 'I'm so hungry, but you look like you're having a rough time of it as well. Do you have any food?'

'Yes, I do,' said the girl, and she shared the bread between them, and went to fetch some river water to wash it down with. They sat on an old tree by the side of the track, and the old woman brightened up a bit.

'Thank you,' she said. 'How can I return your kindness, and help you?'

The girl explained her task with the sieve. 'Do you know the way to the pool at the end of the world?' she asked.

'I certainly do,' said the old woman. 'It's a long time since anyone has asked me about that. You need to travel this road for another day, and then at dawn on the next day, you need to wash your face in dew and turn around three times anti-clockwise. After you've done that, walk through the willow trees in the west, and you will find the pool. What you do when you get there is completely up to you.'

'Thank you,' said the girl, and they smiled at one another before walking on.

She followed the instructions, and eventually found herself squelching through a woodland of ancient willow and alder trees. The mud was deep in places, and sometimes she had to go back and try a different route to get through, always with the sun behind her. Dragonflies whirred around her and willow warblers trilled, as the chiffchaffs encouraged her to go on, go on, to keep trying.

At last, the ground dried enough for her to stand foot-sure and survey the scene ahead.

There in front of her was a pool of water, surrounded by willow trees. When she looked more closely, some of the willow trees had been gnawed away by big teeth, and others were shooting out into leaf again as coppice. At one end of the pond, a big dam of sticks and leaves and mud was holding back the water and stopping it from flowing away.

It was a beaver dam.

Was this the pool at the end of the world?

The girl took the sieve out of her bag. But when she dipped the sieve in the water and drew it out, the water all trickled away. Again and again she tried, but it was no use. It wasn't a magic sieve, even here at the pool at the end of the world.

At last the girl sat down on a tree stump and cried as if her heart would break.

But crying can only last so long, and there is always calm afterwards. When the girl was gulping for air, in the way you do after a really good cry, another voice joined in.

'Ribbit! RIBBIT.'

It was a frog – quite a small frog – crouched at her feet, looking up at her with goggly eyes. His big mouth, turned down at the corners, made him look very wise.

'What's the matter, dearie?' asked the frog.

'Oh, everything's awful, and nothing will ever be happy any more!' cried the girl. 'My mother sent me away to collect water in this sieve, and it doesn't work – of course – because it's a sieve. I can never go home again now. There's no magic in the world after all.'

'Well,' said the frog, 'personally, I'd say that a talking frog is pretty magical ... but, never mind that for now. If

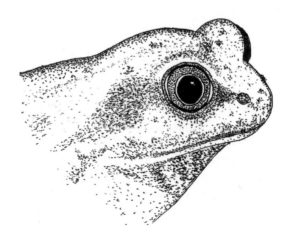

you make me a promise, I'll show you how to fill the sieve with water.'

She brightened up. 'All right.'

'You'll have to promise to do whatever I ask for a night and a day,' said the frog.

That was a bit strange. But why not? 'All right,' she said, 'I promise.'

'Good. Now, look at this beaver dam,' said the frog, 'look how it's been made watertight. That's holding the water back very well. All you need to do with your sieve is to line it with moss and twigs and mud, just like the beaver dam, and it will hold water just fine.'

Then the frog laughed and jumped up into the air, and straight into the pool at the end of the world with a little splash.

The girl's eyes were drying now and she looked around for little things to line the sieve. A bit of sphagnum moss there … a bit of mud, a few tiny twigs, some willow leaves … just there. More moss, and more mud. She pressed it all down into the holes of the sieve, on the base and around the sides.

As she worked, a beaver secretly watched her from the side of the pool, impressed.

The girl reached down into the water with her sieve and then drew it back out. The sieve was full of water, and it didn't leak. The water stayed put. Brilliant!

She smiled and laughed for the first time in ages. The beaver, startled, slapped its tail on the water and disappeared out of sight.

The girl began the long journey home, carrying the precious water in the sieve all the way. As she walked out of that soggy place of trees and mud and life, the frog popped its head out of a nearby pool. 'Don't forget your promise,' it said.

Eventually the girl managed to reach home again, and her mother was very surprised to see her. Secretly she had been missing her daughter, and she was relieved and amazed that she had completed the task that she had set, however difficult. They both drank a little thimbleful of the water from the pool at the end of the world, just to celebrate, and perhaps to bring a little bit of magic to their lives; and the girl told her mother the whole story.

But old habits die hard, and that afternoon the girl was ordered back to her cooking and cleaning duties again, while her mother mended the roof of the cottage. By the time that evening came, they were both exhausted.

They were sitting down and reading after dinner when there was a scraping and scratching at the door.

'Go and see who that is, will you? I can hardly move, my joints are aching so much,' said the mother.

So the girl went to open the door, and there on the doormat was the frog. It said:

> Lift me to your knee, my hinny my heart;
> Lift me to your knee, my own darling;
> Remember the words we spoke
> by the pool at the end of the world.

Her mother laughed. 'Ah, you made a promise! Remember, girls should always keep their promises.'

So the girl allowed the frog to jump on to her hand, and she lifted it up and took it inside. She sat the frog on her knee, and tried not to get too close to the fire, because she could see that would make the frog uncomfortable.

After a while, the frog said:

Give me some supper, my hinny my heart;
Give me some supper, my own darling;
Remember the words we spoke
by the pool at the end of the world.

So the girl fetched the frog a bowl of milk and some bread,
and it fed well.

After it had finished, the frog said:

Take me to bed, my hinny my heart;
Take me to bed, my own darling;
Remember the words we spoke
by the pool at the end of the world.

'But – no offence, you understand – you're a frog,' said the
girl. 'I don't want a cold, clammy frog in my bed.'

The mother roared with laughter, and it wasn't kind
laughter. 'You made a promise!' she said. 'Remember, girls
should always keep their promises.'

So the girl took the frog into the bedroom and placed it
upon the pillow. She got ready for bed, then, and she stayed
as far away from the frog as she could, because it was all a bit
too weird.

Who knows whether the frog slept much at all? The girl
had no idea; she slept well and soundly, after all, despite the
frog on her pillow.

The new day was just beginning to lighten up behind the
curtains, and the girl was just stirring from her slumbers,
when the frog spoke again:

Chop off my head, my hinny my heart;
Chop off my head, my own darling;
Remember the words we spoke
by the pool at the end of the world.

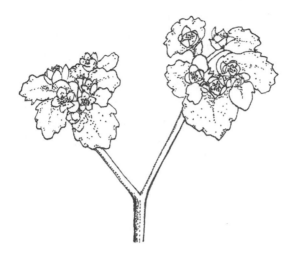

'I can't do that!' cried the girl through the half-light. 'You have been so kind to me, and you have helped me so much. How could I cut off your head?'

He said it again. 'Just for me,' he added.

So the girl went to get the wood-chopping axe from the fire basket. She came back to the bed, and with tears running down her face, she chopped off the head of the frog.

There was no blood. But there, before her, appeared a rather good-looking young man.

'Sorry about the bedroom thing. I'm glad you're wearing your dressing gown,' he said. 'It wouldn't be right otherwise.'

'What happened? I don't understand,' she said.

'Well … it's a long story. In a nutshell, my mother died when I was very little, and my father blamed all his troubles on me. Eventually he said I was useless and changed me into a frog,' said the young man. 'The only way the spell could be broken was if a young girl would do my bidding for a day and a night. He never believed it would happen; but you have proved him wrong. Thank you.'

So the young man and the young woman became firm friends. They shared many stories, much laughter, and a lot of arguments.

Eventually, of course, they got married, and lived happily ever after.

The girl's mother was very pleased for her daughter, and the boy's father – feeling a bit guilty about the frog thing – was very pleased for his son.

Who knows, perhaps the mother and father got together as well. They had a lot to talk about.

6

Breathing Underwater

There will the river whispering run
Warm'd by thy eyes, more than the sun;
And there the 'enamour'd fish will stay,
Begging themselves they may betray.

John Donne (1572–1631)

Fish are magical by their very nature. They can breathe underwater and travel huge distances in their underwater realm, so alien and unthinkable for humans. There are around thirty-eight species of freshwater fish native to Britain and Ireland, and a number of others that have been introduced. Many fish species are in decline because of the deteriorating quality of our rivers, and they suffer particularly from pollution, dams and barriers, and loss of habitat diversity.

In our folk tales, fish inevitably appear as magical crea-tures, able to bestow power, knowledge and gifts. In ancient times, migratory fish such as salmon must have seemed like magicians, disappearing and then reappearing in differ-ent colour or form, following the seasons and jumping the rapids. They are also, of course, a key source of food.

FIONN AND THE SALMON OF WISDOM

The River Boyne is one of the main sacred rivers of Ireland, named after the goddess Boann ('she of the white cow'), with an origin story similar to that of the River Shannon elsewhere in this book. The Boyne rises at Carbury in County Kildare and flows north-east for seventy miles, past the ancient graves of Brú na Boinne (including Newgrange) and out to the Irish Sea.

Linn Feic, a pool on the River Boyne, and the falls of Assaroe at Ballyshannon on the River Erne in County Donegal both claim to be the place where Fionn Mac Cumhaill caught and ate the great Salmon of Knowledge. Assaroe Falls have been destroyed by the construction of a hydroelectric power station, and there is now a fish pass there for the salmon.

The Atlantic salmon is a mysterious and magical fish that travels thousands of miles from freshwater to the sea and back again. Folklore dictates that salmon return to spawn at the very point of the river where they are born, and studies have shown that this is usually true. Nobody quite knows how they do it, although scent and magnetic fields can both be detected by the fish.

Salmon can grow to be over three feet long, and they usually only live for a maximum of six to seven years – if they are allowed to. They need a range of wetland habitats along the river and estuary as part of their complex life cycle. Young salmon also host the larvae of the freshwater pearl mussel, now critically endangered.

Salmon numbers have declined drastically in recent years, and most British rivers now have fewer than half the numbers of salmon they had twenty-five years ago. Siltation and pollution of rivers, habitat loss and over-fishing are all problems for the salmon, and climate change could also be a major threat. Intensive salmon farming creates massive water pollution and problems with parasites and interbreeding for wild salmon populations.

Hazelnuts and salmon are both widely used to represent wisdom in Celtic mythology. In Wales, the Salmon of Wisdom, or Llyn Llyw, swims in the River Severn and is the oldest of all living creatures.

In the very early days of Ireland, it rained and rained, the rivers raged and the waters of the ocean lapped around the foot of the hills and the bogs. Many people and animals on the land perished. But have you ever wondered what a flood would have been like for the creatures under the water?

One great salmon found itself in the sea at the time of the great flood, and his world expanded in all directions. No matter where he swam, the underwater world had transformed, with new gullies and deeps to explore; but when he was called to swim back to the place he had been born, he could not find it. I cannot tell you all the adventures the salmon had, all the strange creatures he met, and all the battles he fought at that time; his silver scales shone and his muscles were lithe, his senses were sharpened and his reactions quickened, by the time the watery world shrank back to something like normal and the tides receded.

Finally, swimming through eelgrass beds and over the estuary mud, the salmon found the place he was looking for: the mouth of a great river, where the salt sea met the clear, cool, fresh water of the River Boyne. Somehow it *smelled* right.

Back in the river now, always swimming against the current, new coppery colours dappled the salmon's flanks as the sun flashed on the gravels below. He swam over great beds of pearl mussels, mouths agape to catch their watery meals; he sensed otters hunting, and twisted away with his powerful tail to hide under the shade of willow trees; he leapt at waterfalls, but he no longer snapped at any flies that landed on the gleaming waters of the Boyne.

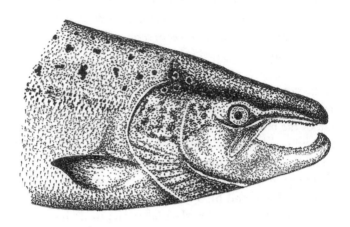

The salmon swam upstream, always upstream for miles and miles, as the river narrowed and babbled and slowed. Right at the top of the River Boyne, he found a deep, still pool in the river, where he could regain his strength.

On the banks, nine hazel trees spread their heart-shaped leaves over the waters of the river pool. Nine hazelnuts hung from each tree, velvety treasures in their spiky green cases. These nuts were filled with all the knowledge of the world.

As the mornings became misty and the mellow colours of autumn fell over the river, the hazelnuts of wisdom swelled and ripened. One day as the salmon was at the water's surface, a hazelnut fell into his mouth and into the salmon's belly; and with that, the salmon found he knew more than he had before.

He waited, and as more hazelnuts fell, he captured them with deft reactions and powerful jaws. Snap! Snap! Snap! All the wisdom in the world, contained in eighty-one hazelnuts, was now contained in the flesh and body of a very fat salmon. His meal complete, and with no desire to be there for the spawning, the great fish swam down, down into the darkness of the pool, out of sight, out of mind, and out of memory ... but not quite.

◎

The years passed, and people returned to the land. Whether the salmon had been seen by some hapless human, or whether the oldest animals had told the secret, tales were told and songs were sung about the great Salmon of Knowledge. They said that if you could eat this salmon's flesh, you would gain all that knowledge. They said that he was somewhere on the sacred River Boyne.

One man, Finneces the Druid, listened more closely to the stories than most. He became determined to find the Salmon of Knowledge; he craved the prize of that fish. Finneces went out to the woods and walked the river, living through the cycle of the seasons, the sun and the rain, the howling winds and the harsh frosts. He used the magic that he knew, the ogham and the calls of the birds, to help him on his quest. That journey led him to the very beginning of the River Boyne, where a dark pool swirled and the hazel leaves whispered in the breeze.

Finneces settled, as much as a wild man can settle in the woods, and in his search for the great salmon he learned much. By trial and error he learned how to hunt, to avoid being hunted, to survive; he learned how to make shelter and how to use fire. But more than anything, he learned river craft, the song of the river in all its moods: the play between air and water, the whistle of the otter and the darting of the mayflies above the river, the battle for light and shade and shelter in the secret places under the surface of a magical kingdom.

As the years went by, Finneces observed salmon in the river at all times of year, and at all ages, from tiny parr to the great glistening hen salmon with their soft, heavy bellies. He worked his magic and imagined himself as a salmon, powerful and sleek, navigating through the waters, asking all he met: where is the great Salmon of Knowledge? He must have fished every single salmon that swam there; he cooked and ate the fish that he needed, and the rest went back to the river, perhaps a little wiser than before.

But he never caught *that* fish, no matter how much he tried, and no matter how much he asked.

In Finneces' seventh summer in the woods, he was joined in the wilderness by an unlikely companion: a member of the Irish warrior clans, and a young one at that. This boy, called Fionn, was running from his father the clan chief, because he had been told that one day his son would grow up to be a greater warrior than he could ever be.

So Finneces now had a willing pupil, and it distracted him for a time away from his salmon-fishing task. Fionn learned quickly, of bardistry, story and song, poetry and language, with nature as his classroom. Finneces was a good teacher, and he enjoyed the company of the lad after being alone in the woods for so long. But every morning at dawn, and every evening before dusk, Finneces made sure to cast his line into the river, somewhere near the deep pool, in the hope of catching his prize. He never told Fionn why he was such a keen fisherman. Fionn, for his part, just thought that Finneces had a really keen hobby.

One day, Fionn's lessons were exhausting. The poems were long and Fionn's attention span was even shorter than usual. By the time the sun was casting long shadows, Finneces had had enough, and both he and Fionn went down to the river to fish.

Fionn's line was the first to go under, and it seemed that he had caught a monster. It took the strength of both of them to haul the fish towards the shore and on to the bank. There on the ground, twitching, covered in dark spots, so heavy it was making a little crater in the mud, was a huge, huge salmon.

Finneces' eyes were wide, and he was so excited he could hardly breathe. 'This could be it,' he thought. 'Finally, here is the Salmon of Knowledge, and all that knowledge can be mine!' He said nothing out loud, but he couldn't help doing a little dance in the mud.

'That's cheered him up,' thought Fionn. But he had no idea of the real reason.

'Don't touch the fish!' said Finneces. 'I'll prepare this one, it needs my skill.' Finneces swiftly filleted the fish, and put it in a pan ready for cooking, while Fionn built a fine cooking fire. The pan was put over the flames.

'I'll go and get the mead to celebrate,' said Finneces. 'Guard the cooking. Whatever you do, don't eat any of it … Promise me, on pain of death!'

Was the old man going mad? 'Of course I won't eat any, I promise,' said Fionn, playing along.

Finneces hurried off into the hazel trees towards their shelter and Fionn watched the salmon as it changed colour in the pan, the sweet red flesh turning dull, opaque pink. As he shook the pan, the salmon's scaly skin crisped and the fat sizzled.

Then a glob of hot salmon fat spat out of the pan and right on to Fionn's thumb.

'Ouch!' Automatically, Fionn put his burned thumb into his mouth.

It was only then that he realised what he had done, because in that bit of hot salmon fat was all the knowledge in the world, and Fionn had just eaten it. Fionn knew where the knowledge had come from; Fionn knew what he would do with it; in fact, Fionn knew everything.

Finneces came hurrying back, and there was the lad sitting by the fire, and the salmon well cooked, but he could see with one glance that everything had changed. Fionn told him about the hot fat from the fish, and Finneces' world turned upside-down as he realised that his past seven years had been in vain.

The Salmon of Knowledge had never been meant for him.

This is what Finneces did next:

First, he gave the salmon to Fionn to eat, and he went without. Perhaps he couldn't stomach it. I wonder if he ever ate salmon again.

Second, he asked Fionn if he could learn some of his knowledge. Finneces was wise enough to understand that Fionn was destined for greatness, and he realised that if he couldn't have all the knowledge in the world for himself, at least he knew someone who did.

In this way, Finneces the Druid showed that he didn't have knowledge, but he did have wisdom.

As for Fionn mac Cumhaill, he became the leader of the Fianna, that band of warrior heroes. Of all of them, he was the greatest of all men in Ireland, perhaps the greatest of all time.

All through Fionn's life, whenever he needed to know about something, all he had to do was bite his thumb.

THE FISH AND THE RING

This story was originally collected in the nineteenth century. Similar motifs can be found in folk tales all over the world. I love the way that the water in this story seems to create all the fated events, despite the baron's dastardly attempts to cause death by water. After all, isn't he supposed to be the one who believes in the fates?

There was once a baron who lived in great splendour and comfort in a castle near York. He was a learned man who was interested in everything, whether it be science or superstition, and he was well known for an interest in fortune-telling.

When the baron's first son was born, he couldn't help but wonder what the fates had in store for the child. His son was barely five years old – a good enough age to answer questions, thought the baron – when, on Midsummer's Eve, the Baron dealt his tarot cards, consulted his magical oracles, and cast the boy's horoscope to find out something about his future.

He checked the cards again. This couldn't be right! The boy was to marry, and happily, but … his beloved would definitely come from humble origins. The girl had just been born, apparently, to a couple who lived in poverty, in a little house just below York Minster, and she already had five brothers.

The baron's face soured. This was no match for his family! He wanted his son to make something of himself, to be ambitious and to get ahead in the world. So the baron decided to make sure it couldn't happen.

The following day, he rode into the city of York on his fine black horse, along the cobbles towards the great cathedral, when he spied a poor man sitting on the doorstep of a little hovel, holding a child in a shabby christening shawl. The child's face was a little screwed up red ball of discontent, and she was wailing so loudly it rang around the alleyways.

The baron stopped and called down to the man. 'Sometimes you can never get them to be quiet, eh?'

'I don't know, sir,' said the man. 'She's already got five brothers, so the poor little mite has no chance. We can scarce afford to feed her. No wonder she's crying.'

'Aww.' The baron tried to look sympathetic, and then smiled. 'I can help, if you'll allow me. I could take her on, so you don't need to worry. What do you say?'

The man brightened. 'Oh, sir, would you? That would give her a much better chance for a good life, and it would take the pressure from us. We'd be very grateful, I'm sure. Let me get my wife.'

An hour or so later, the baron on the fine black horse was galloping out of York carrying a screaming, filthy baby girl. He followed the river downstream from the city until he reached a secluded spot surrounded by trees, where he knelt down by the river bank and placed the child in the shallow water.

'That's the last my family will see of you,' he muttered, as he galloped away towards his castle and his own children.

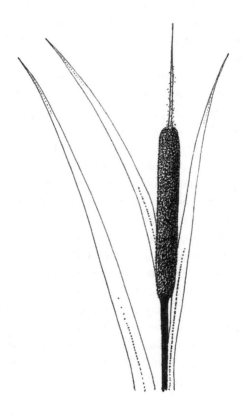

∞

When the baby felt herself surrounded by cool, calm water, glittering in the midsummer sun, she stopped crying, and the gentle ripples of the river against the bankside lulled her to sleep. It wasn't long before the current caught her christening shawl and, with the fabric billowing out around her like a raft, the tiny baby floated downstream, fast asleep and blissfully unaware of the danger she was in.

Several miles further down the river, a fisherman was by the water when he saw a white shape tangling in the reeds nearby. He waded out to discover the little girl still asleep, and he hurried back to his wife with the precious bundle wrapped in his coat.

The fisherman and his wife raised that girl as their own, and she had a happy childhood learning about the river and living simply in their fisherman's hut. The little girl grew into a strong, glowing young woman.

∞

One day many years later, the baron and his friends went hunting along the banks of the River Ouse. It had been a hot day and the whole company was thirsty when they reached a little fisherman's hut and asked for refreshments.

The fisherman and his wife obliged for a modest payment, and a beautiful young girl brought the drinks out to the waiting men on horseback.

'You're a handsome one,' said one of the men to the girl. 'I wonder who you'll marry, then, eh?'

The girl blushed and looked down.

'Baron, you're the one who sees into the future: tell us the fate of this little beauty,' teased another man, turning to the baron.

The baron snorted. 'Oh, some yokel or another, I'm sure. Don't be bothering me with trivia!'

But his friends teased and teased him, until at last the baron turned to the girl.

'All right, all right. I'll cast your horoscope. But I will need to know: what is the date of your birth?'

The girl gave a little curtsey. 'I don't rightly know, sir. My father always says he fished me out of the river, but I never knew if I should believe him.'

The baron felt a little knot of guilt tighten in his belly. 'Oh, I'm sure he's joking about that … Tell me, how many summers old are you?'

'Fifteen, sir,' she said.

The baron knew who she was, then, but he didn't tell.

'Come on, friends, drink up,' he cried, calling to his friends, 'there's more hunting to do!' They all galloped away, but the baron contrived to double back and return for something he'd forgotten; and he called to the girl, now washing the cups by the fisherman's hut.

'Here, girl!' he said, waving a scroll of paper. 'I know you probably can't read, but I like you all the same, and I want to give you a chance. Take this letter to my brother at the big house at Scarborough, and you will be sure of a good job. Here's money for the journey, too.'

The girl took the scroll of paper and small bag of coins and thanked him with another little curtsey, and the baron turned his horse and went to re-join the hunt.

∞

The girl put on her travelling cloak, and took the blessings of her parents with her as she set off on the long journey to Scarborough with the letter still rolled up in her pocket. There was several days' journey ahead by foot, and that evening she found a little inn to stay the night. She ate a good meal at the bar and then went upstairs to her room, where she was soon fast asleep. It had been a long day's walking.

The girl hadn't noticed two pairs of wily eyes watching her at the bar that evening. Two robbers were also staying at the inn, and they were always on the lookout for thieving opportunities. Later that night they crept into the girl's room while she was asleep, and took her cloak and bag back to their own quarters.

'There's nothing here but a scroll of paper and a few coins,' complained one, rifling through the girl's bag.

'What's the scroll of paper say then? You're the one that can read,' said the other.

The first robber unfurled the paper and read aloud:

Dear Brother – take the bearer of this letter and put her to death immediately. Yours affectionately, Humphrey.

'That's not very nice is it?'

'What a pity – such a nice young girl too,' said the second burglar. 'I think we should do her a good turn. Can you get some paper, pen and ink from somewhere?'

It wasn't long before the first burglar was scratching out another letter on a bit of paper from the inn. 'Mind you get the signature looking the same,' said his friend.

They crept back to the girl's room with her cloak and bag, which contained their replacement letter. The original letter from the baron went on the fire. The girl was still fast asleep.

࿓

Several days later she walked into the courtyard of a grand stone house at Scarborough, and wondered at the tall turrets and grand carriages. The only other person in the courtyard was a young man, who walked over to her and smiled at her wide clear eyes.

'Good morning, young lady, what's your business here?'

'I was told to give this to the baron's brother and I would be able to stay here.' She handed him the scroll of paper from her bag.

'Oh, I can do that: I am the baron's son, and I am a guest here at my uncle's house. Please, come this way; you must be tired after your journey.' He showed her to her rooms, and then as soon as he left her he couldn't help but open the letter. He read:

> Dear brother, the bearer of this letter should be married to my son immediately. Yours affectionately, Humphrey.

'Well,' thought the baron's son, 'my father told me he'd find me a wife soon – he doesn't hang about! She is a pretty young woman, and I could do a lot worse. I really rather liked her.' He hurried to find her again and talk some more.

The wedding preparations started that day, but the baron's son and the girl were deep in conversation, walking the woods and the fields and laughing a lot. Within a couple of days the baron's son had given her one of his mother's little gold rings, by way of engagement; and there was excitement at the big house as decorations were made and food was prepared for the big wedding day the following week.

Then the baron himself arrived at the house, and soon learned why the preparations were being made. He was an intelligent man, and he knew better than to cause a fuss; so he listened to his son's raptures about the girl, and then announced that he would take the girl riding and walking 'to learn more about her'.

The baron led the girl out to the coast path along the cliffs at Scarborough. Some way along the path, in a spot where he couldn't be seen, the baron turned to the girl and caught hold of her by the wrists. She screamed with fright.

'This time, you won't get away,' he said. 'This time, it's the sea for you, my girl.'

'Please! Please don't harm me,' she said. 'I don't know what I have done to deserve this, but if you let me live I will do whatever you wish – I will never see your son again unless you want it to happen.'

Her eyes were full of pure terror, and the baron finally felt a pang of guilt at his behaviour. He saw his wife's ring on the girl's finger, and said, 'Give me that ring.'

She pulled the golden ring from her finger and put it in his hand. He hurled it out into the waves.

'Never let me see your face until you can show me that ring,' he said, and let go of her bruised wrists. 'And that will never happen. I will tell my son that you have decided against marrying him. Now get out of my sight.'

෮

Tear-soaked and bewildered, without a penny piece to her name, the girl wandered along the coast path for miles. The path turned inland and she walked for days, scavenging and sleeping in ditches and poor houses, until she came to another grand house where she got a job as a scullery maid, and occasionally as a cook.

A year went by. Then one day, the servants at the house were told to prepare a great banquet for a special guest. The girl happened to be looking out of a high window as the baron and his brother rode into the courtyard, and her heart beat faster as she saw the baron's son on horseback behind them, looking every bit as handsome as she remembered.

But it was no good, she was just a scullery maid, and it was complicated and awful to be reminded of her poor treatment. The girl decided it was best to stay out of their way in the kitchen; they would leave soon enough, and then she wouldn't have think about them any more.

She went back down to the kitchens, and the cook gave her the task of gutting, cleaning and preparing a huge salmon that had been caught that day for the feast. She took a knife and slit the silvery belly of the great creature, cutting into its pink flesh, and then cursing as she realised she had cut too far and into the stomach. She opened up the fish, and there among the entrails of the poor beast was a flash of gold.

It was the ring that the baron's son had given her the year before; the same ring that the baron had thrown from the cliff top. She washed it until it sparkled and put it on her finger, then she carried on working.

That salmon was cooked to perfection, with a piquant sauce and just the right seasoning. She sent it up to the dining hall with the serving girls, and soon one of them returned.

'They love it,' she said. 'They want to meet the cook who prepared such a fine dish. Aren't you the lucky one!'

'Perhaps,' thought the girl as she took off her cooking apron, washed her hands again and went upstairs to the dining hall. She walked over to the table towards the baron's son, who gasped as he recognised her face, and she couldn't help but smile.

'Father! We have found my love! I never believed that she had changed her mind,' said the baron's son.

The baron's face was all over thunder, but the girl walked up to him and showed him her hand, with the gold ring on her finger. 'I will say nothing more of what has happened,' she said, 'but here is the ring.'

They say that people who work with magic and fortune-telling can be very wise, or very arrogant. It was in that moment, I am happy to say, that the baron chose correctly:

he took the girl to a seat next to his son and announced to everyone that she was his son's true wife-to-be.

Of course, the girl and the baron's son lived happily ever after. Even the baron himself couldn't help being a little bit impressed with his new daughter-in-law.

APPY AND THE EEL

Eels are curious creatures. These migratory fish travel huge distances from river to sea and back again, and much of their life cycle is still a mystery even today. European eels are now critically endangered, with numbers reduced by over 90 per cent today compared with the 1970s, because of over-fishing, hydroelectric schemes and other river barriers, and also climate change.

Talking of eel mysteries ... this is an old Romany story that needs to be told as much as possible. It was originally collected from a gruff Manivel Smith in Burton upon Trent by T.W. Thompson in the early twentieth century, and Thompson suspected the teller was embroidering the story, just a little. The first time I heard a version being told, by the indomitable Sharon Jacksties in Ely's at Langport, I almost believed it.

Appy got an eel. He got a big fat eel, from a bloke who worked at the brewery in town. When he got the eel home, he put it in the wash tub to swim about a bit, and then he got on with his meal.

After tea, Appy's missus said, 'I must do some washing.' She came down from the bathroom screaming.

'Oh,' said Appy, 'I forgot I put an eel in the washtub.'

'Well, you'll just have to take it out then, won't you?' she said.

Appy took out the eel, and he couldn't think what to do with it, so he put it in his pocket. To be honest, it had been a long day and he was thirsty, and he had his mind on the pub, four fields away from the house. So up he got and went.

Once he got there, Appy listened to the joyous sound of his first pint of beer being poured, and after the head had settled he took a long draught of beer from his tankard, put it down beside him and began to talk to his mates.

A while later on, when Appy turned back to drink again from his tankard, it was empty.

Someone had been taking his pint! Nobody would own up to it though. After a bit of a scuffle, Appy bought himself another pint and settled down to the conversation – this time with his hand over his tankard.

A while later on, Appy felt something touch his hand – something cold and clammy. He looked down.

It was the eel, out of his pocket and trying to get into his pint!

Appy gave the eel a right smack on the head. 'No,' he said. 'Beer's not for eels. You're a respectable kind of fish, you shouldn't go drinking pints.'

The eel reared up in indignation. 'I've as much right to my beer as the next eel, I'll have you know,' it said. 'I'm not going to be treated like that.'

'Oh aren't you?' said Appy, and he hit the eel several more times.

The eel got angry then. 'Right, if that's the way you're going to treat me, then I'm going home,' it said. 'You'll have to find your own way back over the fields.' The eel went down on the flagstone floor of that pub and it slithered out of the door into the dark.

Appy carried on talking with his mates and had a couple more pints, just because he could, but eventually it was last orders and then he had to go home. Out in the dark, he got through the first field, and was halfway across the second one, wishing there was a moon that night, when there was a noise behind him.

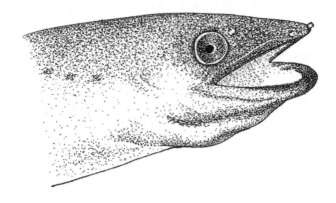

Just a little noise, but it was there, and getting closer, and getting louder.

A rasping, breathing kind of noise.

Appy sped up as best he could, four pints down, but whatever it was behind him was only speeding up and catching up with him.

'Stop,' said a voice. 'Stop, Appy!'

Appy turned around carefully, trying not to fall over, and in the gloom he could just about make out a long, thin shape. It was the eel.

'I waited for you, Appy,' said the eel. 'I didn't want you walking home in the dark, but I must have missed you coming out of the pub.'

'Well, that was kind of you,' said Appy. 'Tell you what, I'll give you a lift home.'

'Thanks – that would be good, I'm tired,' said the eel.

Back at home, Appy got some more water for the bathtub, and the eel was happy in there swimming about.

The next day, Appy was busy, and in truth he didn't give the eel much thought. By late afternoon, he went back to the bathtub, but the eel was gone. He searched and searched, and his missus knew nothing about it. It was a mystery, the disappearance of the eel, and Appy felt a bit sad about it.

Later that evening, Appy walked over the fields again to the pub, opened the door, and there was the bar in front of him. Sitting up at the bar, happy as you like, was the eel, tucking into a pint of beer.

'Evening,' said the eel. 'Pint?'

'Wouldn't say no,' said Appy. The landlord fetched two pints.

'That'll be half a crown, Mr Boswell,' he said.

'What?' said Appy. 'That's expensive beer!'

'Not for the eight pints this 'un has already had, plus these two as well,' said the landlord, winking and nodding at the eel.

'It's true as the gills at me neck,' said the eel. 'True as this pint before me.'

'Well then,' said Appy, 'I'd better pay up then.' And he did.

Time went on, and I'm sorry to say the old eel died eventually. Appy had the eel's skin tanned and he had a fine pair of braces made out of it. The funny thing was, whenever he walked past a pub, the braces started pulling and pulling him through the door, and he couldn't stop them. They were magic braces, for sure.

All this is true, as true as there's eels in the river, and as true as Appy is Appy.

7

THE RAVENOUS RIVER

For life and death are one, even as the river and the sea are one.

Kahlil Gibran 1883–1931

Rivers and people can kill one another. While it is possible for someone to drown in a puddle if they really try, the impact of a river in spate or in flood is really something to be reckoned with. Of course, humans have the capacity to obliterate most living things in a river channel through pollution and dredging, but the sheer elemental force of water will remain nevertheless.

Translated into folklore, this vital energy and force of river water becomes a beast to be feared, to be fought, or at the very least to be respected. Stories of a river demanding human life, sometimes as a regular sacrifice and sometimes in the form of a ghost, occur again and again all over Britain and Ireland. Some tales tell us about rivers as a torrent of emotion, all-consuming and just as deadly. In other places the devil hides under the water, ready to ensnare anyone who is foolhardy enough to investigate.

MAUDLIN MISBOURNE

The River Misbourne begins in Great Missenden in Buckinghamshire, flowing south through Amersham and the Chalfonts, under the railway and through a culvert under the M25, to meet the River Colne and ultimately the Thames. It's a chalk stream, a very rare and precious river habitat. Water levels in chalk streams depend on groundwater, and they can change rapidly, with the upper reaches drying out completely in some years and then returning in winter (called a winterbourne). These days, as with many chalk streams, the Misbourne's flow is seriously threatened by over-abstraction of water for domestic supply in the catchment. More happily, remedial work has recently been carried out on some stretches of the Misbourne and meanders have been reintroduced to the river channel.

This is one of many folk tales about rivers rising up as a warning of bad times to come. It was told to folklorist Ruth Tongue by a Mrs Lee. During a Second World War project run by the Amersham Society, Richard Knight, one evacuee sent to Amersham, recalled being saved from drowning in the Misbourne in 1940. He was lucky to be close to soldiers on a training exercise, learning to cross rivers in their full military kit.

A young woman was riding through the beech woods near Missenden one morning in early autumn, when she was stopped by an old woman with a shawl and a basket and a face made of wrinkles.

'Are you riding down by Misbourne, miss?'

'Well yes, I have been there this morning – the river is unusually full.'

The old woman looked all about her, left and right and behind and ahead.

'Too right it is. My family, we're all heading west. There's danger about, that's what the Misbourne is telling us, terrible danger, black luck. Misbourne says it's coming over from the east.'

'What kind of black luck?'

The old woman shook her head and furrowed her brow.

'When Misbourne rises up and floods, we all know it's a warning, and the worst kind of warning. It flooded when the great plague killed everyone and London burned all to ashes. It flooded when the old king died and there was a great war that lasted four terrible years. Have a mind to Misbourne, miss, she tells of great sorrows in England.'

The old woman shivered and hurried away.

The young woman continued riding through the woods, wondering greatly.

When she got home, she stabled the pony. Just before she got inside, she heard the first sirens filling the air with their wailing, eerie call, prophetic on the breeze.

The Blitz had started.

Lancelot and Elaine

Water carries many things – boats, waste, lives, emotions. The endless movement of water always makes me ponder, more akin to daydream or wistfulness than any notion of logic.

The old English word 'wist' means 'to know'. It's used frequently in Sir Thomas Malory's Le Morte Darthur, *a fifteenth-century bestseller that rambled through the adventures of King Arthur and his knights. Malory's characters are compelling, tangled in a web of courtly love and medieval sensibility. Their stories carry many nuances and questions.*

Astolat was said to be on the same river as Arthur's court at Camelot – and of course, the actual location of Camelot is hotly contested, with claims from many sites across England, Wales and Scotland. Winchester's claim on Camelot probably derives from its status as the capital of Wessex under Alfred the Great, and also Edward I's Arthurian obsession in the thirteenth century; his Round Table still hangs in the cathedral there. The most authoritative version of Le Morte Darthur, *the Winchester Manuscript, was found in Winchester College in 1934.*

Elaine of Astolat is one of the more memorable of the tertiary characters from the Arthurian stories, largely due to Alfred Lord Tennyson's famous 1833 poem 'The Lady of Shallot', which is quoted at the beginning and end of this story. The image of Elaine's body floating down the river to Camelot has been explored by many artists. She is young and vulnerable, she isn't allowed to have her own life and she isn't taken seriously by anyone – her father, her brother, or Lancelot. Would Elaine have been so vulnerable had she not been so protected as she grew up?

It's difficult to find sympathy for Lancelot in this story. You might like to know that after Elaine's funeral, Malory records Lancelot encountering a wild huntswoman in the woods, who accidentally shoots him 'in the thick of the buttock, over the barbs'.

Willows whiten, aspens quiver,
Little breezes dusk and shiver
Thro' the wave that runs for ever
By the island in the river
Flowing down to Camelot.

The River Itchen is a chalk stream, one of those great wild English treasures. Beginning as a shallow, gravelly mass of watercress and floating weeds, the Itchen flows lazily through the great cathedral city of Winchester before meeting the sea at Southampton.

Some say that Winchester was the place of Camelot, the great court of King Arthur and his Knights of the Round Table. It was here that the court would meet, feast together, share counsel and dream of the heroic deeds to come. Among them was the most noble knight, most courageous and most terrible in battle of them all: Lancelot of the Lake.

If you were to walk upstream along the Itchen, along willow-lined banks and through water meadows, further north and further back in time than most of our history records, you would reach another castle: Astolat, towering over the glittering river and the fertile lands and woods beyond.

Many years ago, Bernard, Lord of Astolat, hosted a great jousting contest, and invited King Arthur and his knights to compete. The tents were flapping and the pennants fluttering proudly in the wind as Arthur arrived two days before the festival, with a great and joyous company of men, ladies, squires, pages and other servants; but one knight had decided not to join them.

Back at Camelot, Lancelot was sulking because he had argued with the king; and Guinevere had not travelled to the joust because of a headache. Now here was an awkward situation: queen and knight alone at Camelot, without the king or the court to observe them!

Was this such an accident? Lancelot and Guinevere had long acknowledged their love to one another, but hadn't acted on it, as both of them also held deep love for the king and wanted to cause no scandal or embarrassment to him or to themselves. It was a painful, delicious secret between them.

But unconsummated love has its own way of demanding witnesses.

Lancelot paced the floor of Camelot's great feasting hall, as Guinevere huddled child-like in her throne chair with her skirts wrapped around her.

'I know what our enemies would say,' said Guinevere. 'They will make up all manner of stories against our honour.'

'For sure, they have no respect for the honour of either of us, no matter how innocent we are,' said Lancelot. 'It makes me sick to think of it. I have a mind to joust after all, but as their opponent, not their friend.'

Guinevere's eyes opened wide. 'I would have no fear for your safety, you hold the most skill of all; but would you endanger their lives, truly?'

'This can be a new test of my jousting skills,' said Lancelot, brightening. 'An adventure to wound their egos, but not their bodies. God will assist me.'

The following morning at sunrise, Lancelot rode from Camelot to Astolat, where his horse rattled over the drawbridge just before supper time.

∽

Elaine, Bernard's daughter, was watching from a high window as the knight rode into the castle courtyard, and her heart beat faster as he removed his visor, ruffled his dark hair and looked around with clear, pale eyes. She saw her father greet this stranger with all courtesy, and heard the exchange: the offer of hospitality, the request for a name, and the counter: the knight wished to remain anonymous. Intrigue in the castle! Elaine hurried to braid her pale hair and change into her best gown.

At dinner that evening, Bernard of Astolat's conversation was all about his sons, both now of age: Torre, who had suffered a fall on his first day as a knight and could not ride, and Lavain, who was strong and hearty. Elaine served them with drinks and stole glances at the mystery knight. His smile spoke of experience and foreign lands, and his eyes flashed. Elaine had never seen a man so beautiful in her life, and in the time it took for a jug of wine to be emptied, she gave him her heart.

'As for my beautiful daughter,' slurred Bernard, pulling Elaine close, 'have you ever seen such an example of purity and womanly virtue? She is hardly fifteen summers, and has the full bloom of womanhood ahead of her, with all the fine qualities passed down by her late mother.'

Elaine flushed red and looked to the floor. 'For sure,' said Lancelot, 'you are blessed with fine children, Sir Bernard. I would be delighted if Sir Lavain could ride out with me on the morrow. But tell me more of your son Torre. Do you still have his shield?'

'Yes, although alas he will never be able to use it.'

'May I borrow it? My shield is well known, and in the morning I must parry without being recognised,' said the mystery knight.

Bernard turned to his daughter. 'My dear, fetch Torre's shield for the good knight.' Elaine hurried away, excited to be able to play a part.

She found the shield with its insignia of blue and gold, grabbed a piece of cloth from her chamber, and returned as quickly as she could; but when she walked back into the dining hall, there was nobody there but the mystery knight, wiping his plate and draining his cup.

'Sir,' said Elaine, 'here is the shield. May I look after your shield in return?'

'I would be grateful if you could,' replied Lancelot.

'I will guard it with my life. And ... will you wear a token of mine at the joust tomorrow?'

The knight roared with laughter at this. 'Fair damsel, I have never worn a token of any maid or gentlewoman in a joust. But ... wait.'

The knight pondered. Most of the knights suspected he wore no tokens because of his love for Guinevere. If he wore a woman's token in the joust, then all the other knights would know that he couldn't be Lancelot!

'If I do wear your token tomorrow, know this: it is the most I have done for any maid. What is it?'

Elaine flushed with excitement. 'It is a red silk sleeve, all embroidered with pearls.'

'Bring it to me, then; I will wear it on my helmet for you.'
He smiled at her, and she was dizzy with delight; she fetched
the sleeve, he put it in his bag and then retired for the night,
leaving the room spinning around her.

It was a calm and fair morning with a hint of mist across the
water meadows as Sir Lavain rode out to the joust with their
guest. With armour polished, lances and swords prepared,
and horses and knights fed, the day's jousting began, and it
soon became clear that a mystery knight was stronger than
all. Knights and kings alike fell from their horses – the King
of Northumberland, the King with the Hundred Knights,
Sir Sagramore, Sir Kay, Sir Griflet – all were felled by the
stranger with the red sleeve tied to his helmet.

The Knights of the Round Table turned to one another.
'For mercy,' said Gawain, 'who is that knight? By his riding
and the buffets he deals out, I would say he is Lancelot; but
that good knight never wore a woman's favour, all the time I
have known him, so it cannot be.'

The day continued with many bruises, mostly on Arthur's
side; and as the afternoon wore on, Sir Bors lost his good
humour and rode to challenge the mystery knight; and his
spear cut through the mystery shield and right to the flesh
and ribs, where it remained.

Sir Lavain saw his master fall to the ground and hurried
forward, but the wounded man was already on his feet and
parrying swordplay with Sir Bors. Many crushing blows
were exchanged until truce was called; and then as the trum-
pets blew, the anonymous victor was called before the king.

'Sir,' said Arthur, 'you have fought well of the day, and we
pray you will come with us and join the band of men who
serve this fair land.'

'My lord king,' gasped the knight before him. 'If I have won the day, then it has been sorely bought. I ask your leave to depart from this field and seek medicine, for I am badly hurt.'

Lancelot and Lavain rode away then at a great gallop into the woods. Lancelot stopped in a clearing and groaned piteously, his face white. 'Lavain, can you take this sharp from my side, for I fear if it remains too long it will be the end of me.'

With some persuasion Lavain did as he was bidden, removing armour plates and the offending lance head, and a great flood of bright blood flowed from Lancelot's side. This was staunched as best they could with cloth. 'My lord, what is to be done? I have no healing craft,' wailed Lavain.

'There is a hermit near to here, who is well versed in herb craft,' murmured Lancelot. They rode at a gallop again, with Lancelot's horse streaming and dripping with his blood, until they came to a hermitage, a welcome, and a soft bed for the patient to rest on.

The hermit Baudwin staunched and bound the wound, soothed the knight to sleep with herbs, and turned to Lavain. 'This could have been worse, but it is serious and must be tended,' he said. 'Who is this knight? Is he of the house of Arthur?'

'I know not,' said Lavain, 'save he asked not to be named, but he fought marvellously well against Arthur's side today.'

Baudwin looked again at the patient, and saw a scar on his cheek. 'Ah, now I see his face better and I know it well; this is Sir Lancelot! We shall look after him and nurse him to health, but it will be a long path.'

After some days at the hermitage, and making sure that Lancelot was out of danger, Lavain rode first to Camelot, to tell Arthur and the other knights about the fate of Lancelot. Arthur received the news gravely.

'This was the same knight with no name, who wore a lady's red sleeve into the joust?' he asked.

'The very same, my lord, and the sleeve was from my sister the fair Lady of Astolat,' said Lavain.

'We are grateful for Lancelot's safety, and the one who wounded him will be most pleased of all, for Sir Bors also loves him the best. But we puzzle over Lancelot's battle game against us and the lady's favour he wore; for in all the years I have known him, Lancelot has never worn such a thing,' said Arthur.

Sitting beside the king, Guinevere's face was dark as thunder.

☙

Lavain returned to Astolat and discovered a household worried sick, about him and about the stranger knight, for everyone at the joust had seen how badly he was wounded. Elaine, in particular, ran out to meet Lavain, and begged for news.

'He will live; his life blood has been saved by a skilled hermit,' said Lavain, studying his sister closely. 'But, my sister, look at you so pale: what ails you? Why do you ask so much of the knight?'

'He is my love; he wore my favour on the day of the joust,' said Elaine proudly. 'I give thanks to God that he is safe from death's door.'

Lavain lowered his voice. 'Dear sister, the knight is Sir Lancelot, the most honourable and most skilled knight in the world. That is quite a love to have.'

Elaine barely flinched at the news.

'I do not mind who he is by title; he is my love, and I must see him and nurse him back to health,' she insisted.

When Elaine arrived at the hermitage, and saw Lancelot so pale and sick in his bed, she did not speak, but stayed with him until he awoke. He smiled weakly. 'Fair maid, why do you come here and put me to more pain?'

'Lancelot,' she said, 'I can look after you and bring you back to strength, my love.'

He started. 'Who told you my name?'

'All at Camelot know it: the tale of how you rode in the joust with no name, but carrying my scarlet sleeve,' she smiled.

Lancelot then had little more to say, but much to think on. How could he return to Camelot now? He would have to face Arthur, and explain why he was fighting against his kinsmen. Worse, he would have to face Guinevere, and explain about the scarlet sleeve with the embroidered pearls. He turned his face to the wall and pretended to be asleep.

෮෮

Elaine tended her patient with care, skill and tenderness. Over the weeks and months Lancelot regained his physical strength under her care, but his spirit sagged and he tried not to notice the longing in her touch, or the steady intensity of her gaze. He could not face confronting and upsetting her, he thought, that would be unseemly.

For Elaine's part, she was sure that Lancelot was healing, and in being of service to him she found a steady purpose. Only the hermit Baudwin observed her dedication and cautioned her. 'Guard your heart, damsel,' he said, 'for tender youth can be dashed by those with more worldly purpose.'

Then Sir Bors arrived at the hermitage, and there were words and tears on the part of both men as they bantered and parried and forgave each other their wounds.

It didn't take Bors long to notice. 'Who is this lady who is always at your side? Is it the fair Lady of Astolat?'

'Aye, I owe her a great deal,' sighed Lancelot.

'And you carried her sleeve at the joust? Guinevere is full of anger at that,' said Bors quietly.

'It was part of my disguise, nothing more,' muttered Lancelot.

'She is beautiful indeed,' said Bors. 'Why, will you not marry her? I wish that you could love her – she is clearly devoted to you.'

'That is something I regret,' said Lancelot.

'Well, she is not the first to be devoted to you, and I am sure she won't be the last,' said Bors, and he chuckled.

಄

Bors was a true tonic to Lancelot's spirit, and in less than two weeks he was up and walking; in the same time again, he was in armour and on horseback, and he and Bors were planning on attending another tournament.

First, they would deliver the fair Lady of Astolat back to her family. The two knights rode with Elaine through the woods, until she sighted the great river and her home, her castle next to it. 'How much like a prison it looks,' she thought. 'How much I long for a future with my lord.'

They passed a merry evening of reunion with Sir Bernard, Sir Lavain and Torre; and in the morning Elaine brought all three of them to meet with Lancelot.

'Now, I see you will depart from me, Sir Lancelot. Courteous knight, have mercy on me.'

'What would you have me do?' said Lancelot warily, already half-knowing the answer.

'I would have you as my husband,' said Elaine.

'Fair damsel, I think you heartily, but I cast me never to be a wedded man.'

'Then,' she said, 'will you be my paramour?'

'That would be evil reward to your father and brothers for the kindness you have shown me.'

Elaine took a deep breath. 'Then,' she said, 'I must die for your love.'

Lancelot took Elaine's hand in his, and found it trembling. 'Maid, you shall not do that,' he said. 'You are kind and strong. This I can do for you: that when you find a good knight to wed, I shall yearly give you gold enough for you and your heirs to live in good keeping for the rest of your lives. This much I can give you for your kindness.'

Elaine pulled her hand away. 'To be paid! To be paid! You do not understand. My days are done.' She fell down into a swoon and was carried away by her maids to her chamber.

Lancelot looked up to Sir Bernard. 'I am sorry. She is a fair damsel, and I hope she has a happy life once she forgets me.'

Lavain spoke then. 'Sir Lancelot, since I first saw you in battle, I could not depart from you and I had to follow you. That is the effect that you draw from all you meet.'

Lancelot, embarrassed, left Astolat and rode for the day back to Camelot and the wrath of Guinevere. He had faced it before, and he always won the day.

❦

Elaine made great sorrow then, by day and by night. She didn't eat, or drink, or sleep, and always she complained of Sir Lancelot to anyone who would listen. The bloom in her cheeks faded and her flesh wasted to her bones, until she was so feeble she had to take to her bed.

On the tenth day of Elaine's fasting her father went to her. 'You must leave such thoughts,' he said. 'You are putting yourself in grave danger, and all the youthful promise of your allotted time you throw away, causing all of us deep grief.'

Elaine fixed her father with a steely stare. 'Am I not an earthly woman? I am committing no offence, and I never loved anyone but Sir Lancelot out of measure, and may the Lord have mercy on me for it.' She asked her father to scribe a letter that she dictated, and left him instructions for what was to be done with her body. Her father left Elaine's chamber in sorrow, having humoured her wishes but hoping against hope that she would have a change of heart; but the following morning, her body was cold.

In keeping with her wishes, Elaine's body was dressed richly in white samite and placed in a small barge without sail or rudder. Her shining clothes and pale hair were scattered with yellow flag and meadowsweet, and the letter dictated by her father placed in her right hand. As the willow trees whispered to the water, the barge was pushed away from the reeds at the shore and it caught in the lazy current of the River Itchen as it flowed past Astolat.

> Lying, robed in snowy white
> That loosely flew to left and right –
> The leaves upon her falling light –
> Thro' the noises of the night
> She floated down to Camelot.

By chance, King Arthur and Queen Guinevere were talking together at a window of Camelot Castle when the queen saw a flash of white on the river. Sir Kay was sent to investigate, and three knights hauled the barge from the river in wonder and sadness. Elaine's hair was mingled with water crowfoot now, and blue-striped damselflies flitted over her fair face.

Arthur and Guinevere were called to the river's edge and Arthur spotted the letter in Elaine's hand. 'Perhaps this will tell us more of this poor young woman's fate,' he said, and gently prised her fingers from the roll of paper. He unrolled it and read out loud:

Sir Lancelot, good knight, I was your lover,
men called me the Fair Lady of Astolat.
Pray for my soul, bury me and offer me my mass-penny,
I died a clean maiden, who ever loved you truly,
Yet now my love is dead and washed away.

They all wept then, the king, the queen and the three knights; and Sir Lancelot was sent for.

'You might have shown her some gentleness that could yet have saved her life,' said Guinevere, with a withering look to her own would-be lover.

'Madam,' protested Lancelot, 'she loved me out of measure, and not by my doing. She would not be answered by anything apart from marriage, and that I could not supply. For, madam,' and here Lancelot looked up to the queen with pleading eyes, 'I do love, not to be constrained by love, but to be set free by it.'

'You speak truth, sir, that much is plain,' said Arthur crisply. 'It is your task to do right now by the death of this maiden and see that she is put to rest with all due respect and ceremony.'

The following morning, Elaine's body was interred and Lancelot offered her the mass penny. He prayed for the rest of the day with the other knights in Camelot's chapel.

But down at the water's edge, Guinevere and her women made their own prayers that Elaine's young soul would find peace, as the River Itchen made its sleepy way from Astolat down to the sea.

THE DEVIL AT HAGBERRY POT

The estuary of the River Ythan in Aberdeenshire is possibly the most studied food web in the world, thanks to the work of countless students at Aberdeen University and the nearby Culterty field centre. Gight Woods, an ancient woodland on the steep slopes near to Gight Castle, was the subject of my masters dissertation in historical ecology back in the early 1990s. It is now a Scottish Wildlife Trust nature reserve. I remember towering cliffs, huge wych elm trees and red squirrels, a bees' nest in the dense bur-reed on the floodplain, and a dark, lifeless conifer plantation on the other side of the river.

I also remember being told at the time there was treasure guarded by a devil at Hagberry Pot, although I didn't dare to look too closely. The treasure is said to belong to a laird of Gight who hid it from Covenanters in the seventeenth century. Gight Castle, reputedly the birthplace of the poet Byron, holds many stories. Thomas the Rhymer predicted: 'At Gight three men by sudden death shall dee, And after that the land shall lie in lea.' The castle is now a ruin.

'Loon' is the Doric (Aberdeenshire) word for boy. It also happens to be the other word for a diver, a bird that has a mournful piping call.

On the River Ythan, at Gight just below the castle, there is a deep pool in the river called Hagberry Pot. If you can bear to look, you will see the water swirling around in anger, trying to lure you in – for they say there is great treasure there, guarded by a demon.

Many hundreds of years ago, there were two rival clans at Gight, and they got to sparring about Hagberry Pot. One clan challenged the other to go into the river and see what was there. 'There's treasure to be had,' said the clan's father, 'but only for the brave: let's see who has the stoutest heart!'

Well, there was a challenge. The oldest of the two brothers in the other clan took up the challenge. With all the others crowded around on the river bank, he stripped off to his undergarments and dived straight into the water.

They all waited. For a while, there was nothing but bubbles in the water ... and then, as it cleared, they could see a long stone stairway reaching down, down into the deep. Did it go under the water to the castle on the other side?

It was a good ten minutes before the older brother returned, wading up the steps and gasping for air. He was white as a sheet and whimpering, with bloody cuts all over his face and body.

'What happened, young loon? You don't look so brave. Did you see the treasure?' asked his father.

The lad nodded, but had no words.

'Look at ye,' cried his father. 'Our clan's made of braver stuff. Get back down there and fetch the treasure.'

But the lad refused. Nothing they could say or do would persuade him to go back.

'I'll go,' said his younger son, looking at his brother with a mixture of shame and derision. 'I've always been the braver one. I'll do it.' He stripped off his outer clothes and jumped into the river.

Ten minutes later, the younger brother was sitting on the river bank white as a sheet, covered in cuts and bruises and gibbering. 'It's a devil down there! The Devil himself!'

The other clan saw their chance to prove themselves. It was their only son, a piper, who stepped forward.

'I'm not afraid. I'll go down there, so listen out for me,' he said quietly. 'If it is the Devil, or something's not right, then I will play a lament. If everything's all right, I'll play a pipe march.'

Down he went into the river with his pipes.

They waited, and they listened, and they waited.

About fifteen minutes later, as the water swirled, the sound of pipes began, muffled by the water, but definitely pipe music. As the water rushed along, the sad notes of a lament mingled with the river water.

He never came up to the surface again, that young piper.

But they say that if you wait by the River Ythan at Gight, where the water swirls around in a deep pool at Hagberry Pot, then you might hear the sound of pipes coming from the water, playing a sad, sad song.

PEG O'NELL

Britain and Ireland are full of tales of malevolent river spirits, usually female, who try to drag unsuspecting victims into the water and out of their depth. Some say such stories are nothing more than stern warnings to youngsters about the danger of rivers; others say they are handy tales to explain awkward disappearances and local fears.

Northern England's dark river spirits include Nelly Long-arms, the Grindylow, Teeside's Peg Powler, and most evocatively Lancashire's Jenny Greenteeth, cloaked in slime, breath stinking of sewage, her hand crooked and waiting for unsuspecting ankles. (The ubiquitous duckweed that covers ponds with green is also called Jenny Greenteeth in parts of northern England.) The stories around these characters are usually short, describing a lucky escape or an ugly tragedy – some happen in towns and some in the countryside. They remind me of those 1970s public information films, more akin to horror films, when you tried to guess which child would come to harm first.

The notion of malevolent things in the water is no fairy tale, of course. Nearly all rivers in Britain and Ireland suffer from pollution to a greater or lesser degree, mostly from agriculture, sewage and industry. Although some urban communities have really cleaned up their industrial rivers in recent decades, else-where pollution is getting steadily worse as farming methods intensify, development increases and governments neglect to prosecute polluters.

Our modern, real-time pollution demons are largely hidden out of sight; they are only noticeable if you go near the river at certain times, or try to swim in the filthy water, or look at the data on how our river wildlife is declining. Pollution means death for many living things, intended or not. Sometimes our folk tales just tell it like it is.

This old tale of Peg O'Nell from Yorkshire follows a similar theme.

Peg O'Nell worked at Waddington Hall, near the River Ribble. She had an attitude on her, did young Peg, and she wouldn't take orders well.

One day Peg had a stand-up row with her mistress, and they used all kinds of awful names. Her mistress sent her to the river to fetch water. 'I wish you'd break your neck on the way, you little hussy!' the mistress called after her as Peg flounced out of the kitchen.

That evening, Peg slipped in some muck on the stones near the river, and she did break her neck.

After that, Peg's spirit haunted the river every day.

First were the shrieks and wails coming up from the water, and they meant that nobody at the hall could sleep. Tempers didn't improve at that.

Then came the accidents, each one of them blamed on Peg's ghost. Anything to do with the river seemed to go wrong, and a lot of things at the hall as well. They made everyone fearful of when the next accident would be.

Eventually one of the accidents led to a loss of life, just like Peg's did, and then the old ghost calmed down a bit.

Seven years after that one, there was another accident and another poor person was killed.

Seven years after that again, the lord of the hall took matters into his own hands. When it was coming up to the anniversary of Peg's death, he announced it would be known as 'Peg's night'. He killed a chicken that night – sacrificing a life, so that someone of Peg's choice would not be an unhappy victim.

Many years later, a young man stayed late drinking at the nearby inn. He left after midnight, saying that he had to be at Clitheroe before daybreak.

'You can't do that, sir,' said the barmaid. 'It's Peg O'Nell's night tonight, and there's been no sacrifice, not since the new lord came in. Stay here and be safe, I beg you.'

But the young man laughed. 'Superstitions!' he cried, and set off on horseback.

He must have tried to ride over the ford at the Ribble. The following morning, both horse and rider were found drowned.

Peg O'Nell had taken what she wanted.

8

FLOOD AND FUTURE

There is a tide in the affairs of men
Which, taken at the flood, leads on to fortune;
Omitted, all the voyage of their life
Is bound in shallows and in miseries.
From Julius Caesar, *William Shakespeare (1564–1616)*

Sometimes it feels like there is an endless, silent battle going on between humans and the water environment. People work hard to tame the land, control water, abstract water, introduce new species, kill the species we don't want, and discharge all our waste into the river. All the time, our rivers and wetlands are responding and trying to return to a dynamic natural system that can flood when it needs to do so.

We live in acute and demanding times, and our river environment is in a worsening state. We have the ability and the knowledge to restore our river systems and to control and reverse some of the damage done, but a huge effort is needed by those who manage the land and our water supplies to put this knowledge into action.

In the meantime, our rivers are starting to retaliate. Climate change is bringing more extreme weather conditions to Britain and Ireland as to other parts of the world, and flooding is more frequent, risking lives, crops and livelihoods. This flood risk can be managed to a certain degree through drastic solutions: dredging and barriers. Alternatively, we can choose to farm some land in a less intensive manner, and woodlands and wetlands can be used upstream to make the river system more resilient to flooding. This approach works with nature, not against it, to the benefit of river wildlife as well as humans.

These are the new stories, fed by hope, the courage to change, and the drive to take positive action. The people and organisations who are working hard to achieve wilder, cleaner, more flood-resilient rivers deserve our wholehearted support.

Here are some of our old tales, to provoke thought about our past and future relationship with rivers, wetlands, the plants and creatures that are part of these natural systems.

TIDDY MUN

Some land in Britain and Ireland seems to be made of more water than earth, waterlogged and low lying. Our history and folklore of these places reflects a long battle between people and water that stretches far beyond the river channel itself.

The word 'carr' is derived from the old Norse 'kjarr', meaning swamp. The River Ancholme in the Lincolnshire Carrs once flowed through a shallow valley of marshlands and fen to the Humber estuary. Before engineering works began, the Ancholme valley was flooded for much of the year, dotted with osier, willow and alder, reed beds and marsh. Land could be grazed with cattle in the summer months when the water levels were lower. The river was full of fish and eels. Birds such as curlew and lapwing (peewit) would have been plentiful, with snipe drumming during the summer, teal and wigeon whistling in winter, and warblers and buntings in the reeds. The whole place must have been bursting with life and sound and buzzing with insects.

The Ancholme was straightened in the early 1600s, the first of many attempts over the subsequent centuries to drain the marshes, reduce flooding, improve navigation and make the land more workable for agriculture. It's one example of the systematic draining and 'improvement' of huge areas of low-lying land in England over many centuries, often by command of Parliament, and usually carried out unscrupulously by powerful landowners with little concern for the fate of the local people or wildlife. Drainage didn't always bring positive results. It meant that many of the old farming ways were no longer tenable, leading to problems with animals and disease as the ecosystem was thrown out of balance, and the local people had to adapt where they could.

Let's not be too romantic about the undrained Fens, though – there is no doubt that life in the wetlands was tough, and poverty and prejudice were commonplace (witch-blaming is mentioned in this story). Flooding was a constant threat, and it was difficult to make a living from sodden land. Ague – or malaria – was rife, causing intense shivering and pain in the limbs. The popular 'cure' – opium – was highly addictive and caused more shivering and early death, although it probably did interesting things to local imaginations! Another local cure for ague was to swallow live spiders. At the beginning of the seventeenth century, Thomas Mouffet, father of Little Miss Muffet of nursery rhyme fame, prescribed 'a spider gently bruised and spread upon bread and butter to be taken three times a day as a preventative against agues'. No wonder Patience Mouffet hated spiders.

Tiddy Mun is an extraordinary, heartbreaking story, first recorded by folklorist Marie Balfour in 1891. She heard it from an ageing woman, who said that she had followed the old rituals when she was young. Balfour noted, 'Drained cars like these lie along the wide shallow valley of the Ancholme, between the parallel ranges of the Wolds and the Cliffs … they are still worth seeing … stunted willows mark the dyke-sides, and in winter there are wide stretches of black glistening peat-lands and damp pastures.'

Even when water levels were more controlled, some element of wetland wildlife would have remained in the late 1800s, until more recent years when the efficient machine of industrialised agriculture put paid to it. I wonder what Balfour would think of modern arable farming, with its sterile soil, pesticides and lack of any wildlife for miles.

However, efforts are being made in places to regenerate something of the wildness of the Fens. Raising water levels again, and bringing back Tiddy Mun, is challenging when all the land around has shrunk back for lack of water. If you get the chance, visit projects such as the Great Fen Project and countless nature reserves owned by Wildlife Trusts and RSPB across the eastern counties, and you will gain some idea of what the original marshlands must have been like.

As for the marshland spirits: todlowries are a local kind of fairy or hobgoblin, while boggarts are an altogether more disagreeable and disgruntled creature. Will-o-the-wisps, or marsh lights, are a natural phenomenon caused by marsh gases.

I've retained some of the original dialect collected from the old woman who told this story to Marie Balfour, because the words are beautiful and resonant of place.

In the old days before the dykes were dug and the river bed was changed, when the land was nothing but bogs full of water holes, the Carrs were teeming with wild and evil spirits. There were boggarts and will-o-the-wisps, voices of dead folks, and hands without arms that came out of the dark pools, crying and beckoning all night through;

there were todlowries dancing on the tussocks, and witches riding on the great black snags, and evil snakes writhing in the water. It wasn't a place to be outside in the dark of night.

Of course, people who lived in the Carrs knew about the spirits and they wouldn't go out at night without a charm of some sort. They shook with fright when they found themselves in the Carrs at darklings; but that wasn't the only thing that made them shake, for the ague was every-where. Men, women and children alike shook from head to foot in the Carrs in those days. They were weak with fever, and many of them were fit for nothing but drinking gin and eating opium.

But not all the sprits were evil. Everyone knew about Tiddy Mun. He lived in the deep green still water holes, and only came out in the evenings when the mists rose. Then he came creeping out of the darkness, limpelty-lobelty, like a little old grandfather no bigger than a three-year-old with long white hair and a long white beard, all matted and tangled together. Tiddy Mun wore grey, so they could hardly see him in the dark, but they could hear him splashing through the water, limpelty-lobelty, and sighing like the wind, and laughing like the peewit. He wasn't wicked and tantrummy like the water wives, or creepy like the dead hands; but it sent a shiver down your spine nonetheless to hear his screeching laugh, passing in a skirl of wind and water. Everyone crowded a little closer together then, glancing over their shoulders and whispering, 'Listen to Tiddy Mun!'

Mind you, the little man without a name never hurt anyone, and he was very helpful at times. When the year was wet and the water rose in the marshes up to the door-sill, come the first New Moon, father, mother and children would go out in the dark, look over the bog and call out together, scared and shaking:

Tiddy Mun, without a name,
the water's through!

The peewit would screech across the swamp, a sign that Tiddy Mun was calling to them, and so they would go inside; and in the morning, sure enough, the water would be down again. Tiddy Mun had done the job for them.

Maybe it's better now, but maybe it's not, because we have lost Tiddy Mun.

It started when the people came to drain the marshes, some of them from the cities and some from over the sea. They said the mists would lift, the bogs would become firm earth for crops and the ague would leave. They said everyone would be better off.

But the Carr-folk didn't like change, nor did they like the people who brought it. They wouldn't give them food or drink or a bed for the night, or any fair words; nobody would let the draining folk cross their threshold. They said ill times would be coming for the Carrs if the bog holes were meddled with and the sopping, quivering bog was turned into firm ground. Tiddy Mun wouldn't stand for it. Even though the Carr-folk knew that ague came from the bogs, 'Bad is bad,' they said, 'but meddling is worse.'

But there was no stopping the draining work. The dykes were dug, larger and larger and deeper and deeper; the land became as dry as a two-year-old mothering cake; the water ran away, down to the river, and the black soft bog lands were changed into neat, tidy green fields.

Although the work got done, it wasn't without trouble. At night at the inn, on the settle, and around the home fires, strange and creeping tales were told. The old ones wagged their heads, and the young ones wagged their tongues, and they all said the same: bad luck comes if you cross Tiddy Mun! The people who drained the land were disappearing, everyone knew – they were spirited away, not a sight of them anywhere true as death. Tiddy Mun had taken them away and drowned them in the mud holes, where they hadn't drained away all the water – that's what comes of crossing Tiddy Mun!

But more men came to drain the marshes; no matter how many Tiddy Mun took there were always more.

Then things started to go wrong for the Carr-folk. The cattle pined, the pigs starved and the ponies went lame; the children took sick, the lambs died, the crops failed, the new milk curdled, the thatch fell in and the walls burst out. Everything went arsy-varsy.

At first the Carr-folk thought it was witches or bog-garts causing the problems. Many women were accused of witchcraft, stoned or ducked in the horse pond, but still the troubles came. Everyone said 'Our Father' backwards and spat to the east to keep the todlowries from pranking; but nothing stopped the trouble from continuing.

Then they knew it was Tiddy Mun himself who was angered, and he was taking it out on the poor Carr-folks, even though the draining wasn't their fault. The children sickened and died in their mothers' arms, like a frost that came and killed the bonniest flowers. The people's hearts were sore and their bellies were empty from the bad harvest. Something must be done, or the Carr-folk would soon be dead and gone. What could they do?

Someone had an idea then. 'You remember when we used to call to Tiddy Mun, when the marshes were still here and when the waters rose. Perhaps if we called to him again, and gave him some of the water back – and tell him that we would restore it all if we could – maybe he'll take it as a bad spell undone, and forgive us.'

So they came together in the evening at the next New Moon. There was Tom of the Hatch and William, his sister's son from Priestrigg; crooked Fred Lidgitt, and Brock of Hellgate, and Ted Badley; and lots more of them, all with their women and children. They jumped at every sigh of wind, and screeched at every snag, but they didn't need to worry. The poor old boggarts and swamp bogles and will-o-the-wisps were no longer out there.

Every one of them, men and women and children, carried a bowl of fresh water in his hand. They stood at the edge of the dyke, looking over to the new river, and they watched the light fall to the west as the running water lip-lapped at the edges of the channel.

Finally it was truly dark, and they all called out together, strange and loud:

Tiddy Mun, without a name,
Here's water for you,
Take your spell undone!

The water was tipped out of every bowl into the dyke, splash sploppert!

Then they listened, and waited, and listened.

No answer came from Tiddy Mun, there was only silence and stillness, and still they waited. Just when they thought it was no good, a wailing and whimpering came from the land all around them, a sound enough to break their hearts, for it sounded like the cries of all the babies they had lost, with nobody there to comfort them. The sound made the people's hearts ache to hear. The women said that tiny hands touched them, and cold lips kissed them, and little wings touched them that night as they waited and listened for Tiddy Mun.

The cries died away into stillness and silence again, and the water lapped at the edges of the dyke. Then, cutting through the dark, there was the cry of a peewit, loud and shrill. It was the old man's holler; it was Tiddy Mun, answering their call! And the cry was so kind and plaintive and happy, they were sure that the spell was rightly undone.

Everyone there burst into cries of laughter, of relief, running and jumping about as if they were children out of school; and they set off with light hearts, and never a thought of a boggart or a witch. Only the mothers hearkened for the tiny cold fingers and crying voices of their little ones, drifting about and sighing through the night.

But from that day, life thrived in the Carrs. The children heartened, the cattle were strong and the pigs fattened nicely. The men earned good wages, and there was plenty of bread; for Tiddy Mun's spell was undone.

> Tiddy Mun, without a name
> White head, walking lame;
> While the water soaks the fen
> Tiddy Mun'll harm none.

Every New Moon after that, everyone went out in the dark to the nearest dyke edge, father and mother and children; and they all threw fresh water into the dyke, crying:

> Tiddy Mun without a name
> Here's water for you!

And the peewit would call back, loud and tender and pleased.

Those who didn't go out would sicken and pine away until the next New Moon, when all could be put to rights; and many a parent brought the fear of Tiddy Mun's wrath down on a child's conscience, so that they were good as gold.

But those days are long past now. Folk never hear tell of Tiddy Mun, and so they don't know about him, and they don't know what to do when times are bad. Perhaps Tiddy Mun has drifted away, for nobody notices now when the New Moon returns, the land is dry, and the peewits are gone.

THE TWO SWANS

Here's another swan story: an old Romany tale, collected in Anglesey. It cuts through judgement, custom and family problems to demonstrate a simple truth: humans and other creatures can help one another.

This story begins with love.

Nestled into a valley in the hills there was a grand house with beautiful gardens, full of graceful trees, blooming roses and a calm, clear lake. On that lake there were two swans.

The only child at the great house was a young woman, and she had a secret sweetheart. They crept away and met in the hidden places in those gardens. They could keep out of sight beneath the great yew tree, behind the great hornbeam hedges at the edge of the formal flower beds. They could talk and laugh in private, down at the lake where the water curved round and the drooping crack willows hid them from sight of the house, and the gardeners were sworn to secrecy. They met all through the seasons of a whole year.

All her father wondered about was his daughter's sudden interest in the great outdoors. But then, inevitably, one day the couple were wandering starry-eyed down a path in the gardens, when there was her father, and it was too late to hide. He walked up to them both, looked at the young man and scowled.

'I know your face. You're from the village over the hill. And you're not from a good family. How dare you meet my daughter in secret!'

He then turned to his daughter. 'If you ever see him again, be sure that I will banish the both of you, or worse. I have my shotgun, and I'm not afraid to use it.'

And that was that.

Did the two lovebirds listen? Of course not. They were in too deep for that. They carried on, but their meeting places were more secret, their meetings less frequent – and that only made them all the sweeter.

Several weeks later, the lad was creeping through the gardens in the dusk, darting from tree to tree as if he was a burglar, when there was the father again, this time carrying his shotgun.

'I warned you!' he roared. 'Now you'll be sorry!'

The young man found himself running for his life across the fine lawns of that garden towards the lake, with the gun blasting behind him. Thankfully the father wasn't a very good shot: but the lad ran and ran like a startled rabbit along the lakeside, along and along the rushing river that fed into the lake, his heart racing, his life in danger.

Now this river was famous as a dangerous spot. There were no crossing points for at least twenty miles, and the currents were strong. But that meant that her father couldn't cross the river: he couldn't be caught!

The young man, seeing no option, dived into the river and swam for his life. Luckily, he was a strong swimmer and the fates smiled on him; and eventually, legs aching and soaked to the skin, he stood, dripping, on the other shore.

By that time the father had gone back inside the big house with his gun, shaking his head and muttering, 'That'll learn him. He won't be back again.' He went to look for his daughter, not knowing that she had been hidden behind a yew tree all the time, and she'd seen everything. Her first thoughts were to her love.

She searched and searched the garden, also on the run from her father before he caught up with her. Down at the lake, the two swans swam to the point where it met the river, and then accompanied her as she walked along the river as far as she dared.

'I'm over here!' came a familiar voice from over the river. 'It's safe over here, he can't get to us.'

'How can I reach you there? I can't swim,' she said.

Now the river divided them, and the situation seemed desperate. But then one of the swans, ungainly out of the water, waddled towards her and stood on the ground patiently in front of her.

'The swan wants to take you across the river on its back,' he shouted.

'Don't be silly!' she said. 'How could I possibly ride on a swan?'

The swan peered round at her with its graceful neck curving in a question mark, and it ruffled its feathers.

It was worth a try. It wasn't long before she found herself sitting on the back of the swan. Her hands were in soft white feathers and her legs were trailing in the water as the swan paddled through the currents and across the racing water, the other swan gliding alongside. Then, it walked out of the river on the other bank, and she could be in her love's arms again.

Mid-embrace, the sweethearts looked down and there were the two swans, nuzzling each other. The swans waddled back to the water again and swam away.

'We can't stay here: but now's our chance, my love,' said the young man. 'We're free. I know a little old wise man in the hills: he used to be a priest and he can marry us. Marry me now.'

And that's what they did. They climbed up, and up into the hills for hours that evening, the steep paths becoming narrower into the trees, with nothing but the moon to light their way. The wise man welcomed them into his comfortable little home, and in the morning they were married in a woodland glade with nobody but the pine marten and the raven as witness.

Once the vows were said, the marriage was sanctified and the cup of mead was drained, they thanked the wise man and took their leave.

'Where to next, my beloved? Where would you like to live now? We can do anything we want,' said the young man.

His new wife was fretful, and possibly a little more realistic. 'They'll be looking for us everywhere,' she said. 'We'll have to own up at some point. My father will have to accept the binding words of a priest. He'll have to accept our marriage.' But her new husband was worried: he remembered the shotgun.

'Why don't you go on ahead then,' he said, 'and break the news, and get his temper over and done with. I'll follow on afterwards, and perhaps he'll look on me more kindly by then.'

'No, that's not right,' she said. 'What's the use of being married then? We must both go back and face the music, and be brave – for it would be better to be banished together than be parted.'

That was the first argument they had ever had, and of course she had her way.

They went back to the river, worried and jumpy. There on the river were the two swans, looking wise and unruffled. It wasn't long before they were both on the backs of the swans, crossing the currents safely to the other side of the river, which was definitely unsafe.

'Thank you,' she said to the swans. 'You are a blessing to us.'

The two newlyweds walked cautiously, arm in arm, and followed the river's course back along to the lake and the gardens of big house; and the two swans chose to walk with them, one on either side.

When they got back to the lake, they were tired after a big day, and so they got on the swans' backs again. The swans swam out to the middle of the lake and then stopped; and, each of them on the back of a swan, the two sweethearts slept safely and soundly that night, nestled in feathers of pure white.

Next morning they woke early and, carried back to land, they crept through the gardens right up to the house. Around the back, there was a window open and they climbed in. There was a guest bedroom, and, again not feeling quite strong enough to face her father, they climbed into bed and fell fast asleep in each other's arms.

Several hours later, a servant came in to clean the room and found the couple still fast asleep. She didn't wake them, but went to fetch her mistress at once.

The mother popped her head around the door of the guest bedroom and didn't have the heart to wake the two lovers from their slumbers. What should she do? She could see that her daughter had set her heart on this young man, and she didn't want to lose her.

So she went to her husband. 'I've found our beloved daughter, safe and well, with the young man. I know where they are.'

'Where, then? Where are they? We've looked everywhere!'

'I won't tell you, not until you promise they will come to no harm.'

'I'll promise no such thing,' he cried, 'she will be punished harshly for disobeying me, and as for the lad … Tell me where they are, and be quick about it!'

But she refused, no matter how angry he got. Eventually he had to give in and agree to her conditions, and she made him swear them on the good book, just in case.

Then she told him, 'Go upstairs to the second bedroom and you'll find them in bed together there. Seeing as they're together like that, out of wedlock, I think they should be married as soon as possible.'

'By God,' he said, 'I'd string up that young ruffian if I hadn't made my promise to you.' He marched upstairs and flung open the door, and finally they woke up, confused and terrified, dragging the covers up around them in defence.

'You know the treatment that you two should be expecting, me finding you like this?' yelled her father, and they both looked at him in terror.

'Yes,' they both said, looking at him, then looking at each other, not wavering, giving themselves up to their fate.

He saw the look in their eyes, and finally his heart went out to them then: they were a young couple in love. Something inside him remembered the same feelings from so long ago.

There was a pause.

'Lad. I want you to promise me one thing, and one thing only,' said the father, gruffly.

'What … what's that?' said the terrified young man.

'I want you both to go and get married at once.'

'I can't do that,' spluttered the young man.

'What?' cried the father. 'You'd rather I banish you from here and you never see my daughter again?'

'I'm sorry,' said the young man, 'but I can't do as you ask: we are married already.'

'What! And when did that happen, I'd like to know?'

'Yesterday, up in the hills, we were married by a priest.'

'That's impossible. You could never have got across the river; there isn't a bridge for twenty-five miles.'

'Go and ask the swans, father. They will tell you it's the truth,' said the young woman quietly from the bed.

'Talking swans? Do you mean to make a fool of me?' shouted the father. His anger was rising again and he stormed

out of that room, leaving the two newlyweds looking at each other, confused, but also unexpectedly full of hope.

That afternoon the father was in a foul mood, pacing around the house. Eventually, he roared to his wife and nobody in particular, 'I'm going out for a walk.'

He found himself walking down to the lake, and there were the two swans on the water in front of him, calm and serene.

'You're nothing but dumb birds,' he found himself saying to them, 'how on earth could you carry someone across a river?'

'Not as dumb as you think,' said the first swan. 'We know those two, we have been watching them for months.'

'We saw the young man swim across the river,' said the second swan, 'and we wanted to help them. So we carried your daughter across, too.'

The two swans then took off from the lake water towards the river, leaving the father open-mouthed, looking into the sky.

He realised that his daughter and her sweetheart had been telling the truth all along, and for the first time he felt badly about how he had treated them.

The father threw a great wedding party for the newlyweds, and he gave them a big house of their own to live in, further down the river.

They lived well and happily, and they had many children; and on the river, the two swans tended to their cygnets in their nest in the reeds at the water's edge.

This story ends with love.

THE AFANC

Here is another river monster, this time particular to Wales and with a love of flooding rivers. The afanc has been vanquished by many mythical Welsh heroes, including Peredur and King Arthur himself. As this monster trots through Welsh myth, he variously takes the shape of a crocodile, a platypus-type creature, a good old-fashioned devil, or sometimes a beaver. The word 'afanc' actually means beaver in Welsh. (Given that actual beavers are vegetarian and pretty harmless, I think turning them into monsters is very unfair.)

However, this story also talks of flooding as a major problem. Since the beginning of human settlement, people have tried to drain land more and more effectively, both to render it more useful for farming and also to prevent the destructive effects of flooding. From a mythological point of view, any monster linked to waterlogged wetlands, or floodplains that perform their natural function, is going to come into conflict with people who want to tame or control a river system – particularly as the human population grows.

Those working in land and water management at the landscape scale will recognise another theme in this story: retaining water higher up in the catchment. Flooding can be alleviated by storing water in woodlands and wetlands at the headwaters of a catchment, slowing the flow in extreme weather events. At the moment, our over-grazed, bare uplands and eroding peatlands only have limited potential to hold water, and there is much restoration work to do.

This endears me to the poor old afanc, because it is a creature trying to create its own wetlands.. We will meet him more frequently yet, as the weather extremes of climate change increase. The River Conwy is flooding more and more frequently these days, and a new landscape restoration project called 'Tir Afon' has begun. Our future lies in a landscape where we can live alongside flooding, create new wetlands and woodlands to hold some of the water back, and live alongside the afanc in our midst.

At the beginning of things, the people of Wales settled in the valleys and they prospered. In the lowlands, the soil was rich and the crops were successful, and the people multiplied and were happy.

But along the River Conwy there was a problem. In a deep pool just above Betws-y-Coed, a great monster lurked in the deep, and everyone said that it would attack and eat any creature that came near – human, animal or bird. They called this creature the afanc, and the pool was named after it – Llyn-yr-Afanc.

The afanc caused mayhem and flooding wherever it went. Few people actually saw it, but they heard it roar and snarl. Some said it had a flat tail for swimming, others said that it dragged people under water to drown them and store them in its underwater larder. Many heroes tried to kill the afanc, but no weapon could pierce its thick hide.

No matter how much it ate, over time the afanc got angrier and angrier. The river flooded all the time. Crops were ruined, homes were destroyed, and people and animals died in their hundreds.

Something had to be done. The chieftains and the leaders met at Betws-y-Coed and agreed they would move the afanc to a place where it couldn't cause so much damage. A blacksmith was ordered to make the strongest chains that had ever been crafted.

'But,' said one chieftain, 'how do we attract the beast to trap it? What do water monsters get attracted to?'

'I guess it's the same as other river monsters,' said another. 'They are all meant to like young maidens, aren't they?'

Calls were put out across the land for any young maiden brave enough to take on the afanc – and strangely enough, none answered. However, in time, one shy young girl did come forward, and she was asked to put flowers in her hair and go to sit by the great pool where the afanc lived.

The girl was very nervous, and she crept up to the edge of the pool and sat down there under the trees, with flowers in her flowing locks. She didn't quite know what to do next, so she started to sing very softly: a lilting Welsh lullaby.

The song drifted across the water of the pool, and from the depths the afanc started to listen. The music was beautiful! Slowly the creature crept out from the water, entranced, its flat tail dragging on the ground, and it came closer so that it could hear more clearly. The girl, terrified, carried on singing, softly, softly. It wasn't long until the afanc had been lulled to sleep on the bank of the pool, and it started to snore.

They crept up to the great monster then and fastened strong iron chains to its arms and legs and tail. When the afanc woke, he roared and tried to break the chains and return to the water – but ten sturdy oxen had been hooked up to the chains, and they started to pull and pull and drag the complaining afanc out of the pool and across the ground.

Those strong, brave oxen pulled the afanc for a good twelve miles, up the valley and mountain slopes to Llyn Glaslyn, just below the summit of Yr Wyddfa. There, the great afanc was dumped unceremoniously in the cold water and the chains were broken.

The afanc, sulking, retreated to the depths of this new pool and he stayed there. The lake was so deep that even the afanc couldn't cause it to flood, and the rocky sides of the pool couldn't be breached. No birds flew over the water, for fear of being caught and eaten.

Flooding on the River Conwy reduced – at least for a while. The great afanc has lived in Llyn Glaslyn from that day to this.

These days, the afanc eats sheep. Mostly.

STORY SOURCES AND FURTHER READING

Bailey, J. and England, D. *Lancashire Folk Tales* (The History Press, 2014).

Balfour, M.C., 'Legends of the Lincolnshire Cars'. *Folklore* 2, pp.145–170 (1891).

Breverton, T., *Physicians of Myddfai: Cures and Remedies of the Mediaeval World* (Cambria Books, 2012).

Bruford, A.J., and MacDonald, D.A. (eds), *Scottish Traditional Tales* (Birlinn, 2003).

Briggs, K., *A Dictionary of British Folk Tales* (Routledge and Kegan Paul, 1971).

Cooper, H., *Le Morte Darthur: the Winchester manuscript*, Sir Thomas Malory (Oxford University Press, 1998).

Coxhead, J.R.W., *Devon Traditions and Fairy-Tales* (W. Delderfield and Sons, 1959).

Crossing, W., *Tales of the Dartmoor Pixies: Glimpses of Elfin Haunts and Antics* (London, Hood, 1890).

Crossley-Holland, K., *British Folk Tales* (Orchard Books, 1987).

Gibbings, W.W. (publishers), *Folklore and Legends. Scotland* (London, 1889).

Grahame, K., *The Wind in the Willows* (Methuen, 1908).

Graves, A.P., *The Irish Fairy Book* (A&C Black Ltd, 1938).

Gwilliam, B., *Worcestershire's Hidden Past* (Halfshire Books, 1991).

Gwynn, E. (ed.), *The Metrical Dindshenchas*, Volume 3, translated by Isolde ÓBrolcháin. https://celt.ucc.ie//published/ G106500C/index.html. pp. 286–297; poems 53 and 54.

Henderson, W., *Notes on the folk-lore of the northern counties of England and of the borders* (W. Satchell, Peyton & Co., London, 1879).

Holmes, N. and Raven, P., *Rivers: a natural and not-so-natural history* (Bloomsbury, 2014).

Hunt, R., *Popular romances of the west of England; or, The drolls, traditions, and superstitions of old Cornwall* (3rd ed.) (Chatto and Windus, 1903).

Hutchinson, W., *The History & Antiquities of the County Palatine of Durham* (Mr S. Hodgson and Messrs Robinsons, 1785).

Jacobs, J., *English Fairy Tales* (David Nutt, 1890).

Jacobs, J., *More English Fairy Tales* (David Nutt, 1894).

James, M., *Investigating the Legends of the Carrs: a study of the tales as printed in Folk-Lore in 1891* (University of Swansea, unpublished PhD thesis, 2013).

Joiner, C.G., 'The Knucker of Lyminster', in *Sussex County Magazine* III (1929).

Jones, T. Gwynn, *Welsh Folklore and Folk Custom* (Methuen & Co., 1930).

Kingsley, C., *The Water Babies, a fairy tale for a land baby* (Macmillan, 1863).

Leather, E.M., *Folk-lore of Herefordshire* (1912).

Mabey, R., *Flora Britannica* (Sinclair Stevenson, 1996).

MacKillop, J., *A Dictionary of Celtic Mythology* (Oxford University Press, 1998).

Marshall, S., *Everyman's Book of English Folk Tales* (Dent, 1981).

Parkinson, T., *Yorkshire Traditions and Legends* (London, 1889).

Potwin, L.S., 'The Source of Tennyson's the Lady of
    Shalott'. *Modern Language Notes.* 17 (8): pp. 237–239 (1902).

Phillips, N. (ed.), *The Penguin Book of English Folk Tales* (Penguin,
    1992).

Purseglove, J., *Taming the Flood: a history and natural history of
    rivers and wetlands* (Oxford University Press, 1988).

Reeves, J., *English Fables and Fairy Tales* (Oxford University Press,
    1954).

Riordan, J., *Folk-tales of the British Isles* (Raduga, 1987).

Simpson, J., *British Dragons* (Batsford, 1980).

Standring, C., *Amersham World War 2 Reminiscences.* Amersham
    Society newsletter, 2004, unpublished.

Tennyson, Lord Alfred (1833 and 1842) *The Lady of Shalott*
    (versions).

Thomas, W.J., *The Welsh Fairy Book* (Frederick A. Stokes, 1907).

Thompson, T.W., 'Some new Appy Boswell stories'. *Journal of the
    Gypsy Lore Society*, Series 3 vol. 5, pp.120–125.

Tongue, R., *Somerset Folklore* (The Folklore Society, 1965).

Tongue, R., *Forgotten Folk Tales of the English Counties* (Routledge
    & Kegan Paul, 1970).

White, J., *Black poplar: the most endangered native timber tree in
    Britain* (Forestry Authority Research Information Note 239,
    1993).

Yeats, W.B. (ed.), *Fairy and Folk Tales of the Irish Peasantry* (Walter
    Scott Publishing Co., 1888).